"Would you li[ke] some coffee?"

Dangerous. Not wis[e] I still have some wor[k]

Half relieved, half disappointed, Kate reached for the door handle. "I understand."

Cade touched her hand. "Do you understand, Kate?"

"Yes. We're both confused by what's happening between us. Why did you ask me out?"

"You're certainly direct."

"Game playing bores me. It's a waste of time."

"I don't play games, Kate. Why did you go out with me?"

"Because you interest me."

"The timing is all wrong for us, Kate."

"I didn't know there was an us."

"We both know there could be."

Dear Reader,

Spellbinder! That's what we're striving for. The editors at Silhouette are determined to capture your imagination and win your heart with every single book we publish. Each month, six Special Editions are chosen with *you* in mind.

Our authors are our inspiration. Writers such as Nora Roberts, Tracy Sinclair, Kathleen Eagle, Carole Halson and Linda Howard—to name but a few—are masters at creating endearing characters and heartrending love stories. Their characters are everyday people—just like you and me—whose lives have been touched by love, whose dreams and desires suddenly come true!

So find a cozy, quiet place to read, and create your own special moment with a Silhouette Special Edition.

Sincerely,

The Editors
SILHOUETTE BOOKS

MARGARET RIPY
Wildcatter's Promise

Silhouette Special Edition

Published by Silhouette Books New York

America's Publisher of Contemporary Romance

SILHOUETTE BOOKS
300 East 42nd St., New York, N.Y. 10017

Copyright © 1986 by Margaret Ripy

ISBN: 0-373-09351-9

First Silhouette Books printing December 1986

America's Publisher of Contemporary Romance

Printed in the U.S.A.

Books by Margaret Ripy

Silhouette Romance

A Second Chance at Love #71
A Treasure of Love #170

Silhouette Special Edition

The Flaming Tree #28
Tomorrow's Memory #76
Rainy Day Dreams #114
A Matter of Pride #134
Firebird #164
Feathers in the Wind #189
Promise Her Tomorrow #209
Wildcatter's Promise #351

MARGARET RIPY

loves to travel and writes only about places she has visited. In her books there is a "little bit of herself and her experiences." Without the support and love of Mike, her husband of fourteen years, she says her writing wouldn't be possible. He has the characteristics she wants in a male hero.

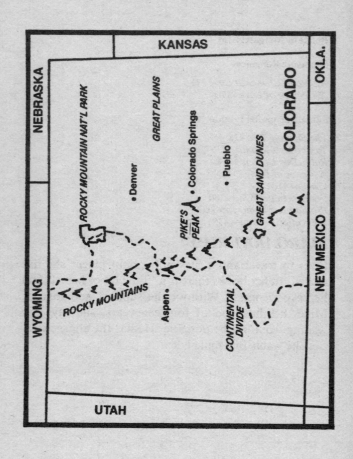

Chapter One

Sunlight bathed the mountains in a blaze of fiery color, promising a beautiful spring day. But viewing the tall peaks with Denver at their feet, Kate felt despondent.

Today was her wedding anniversary, but she had no one to share it with. Those same tall mountains that looked so tranquil now had taken her husband from her the year before. She knew her anniversary would be the hardest day to get through; it had been incredibly hard last year, only four months after Thomas's death.

Again she would immerse herself in her work, determined not to think of the past. But memories crept into her thoughts as she turned her chair away from the window. The fun, the happiness, the love she and Thomas had shared were precious treasures that many people never experienced.

Her life had been wonderful, full of promise like this spring day. It was still hard for her to believe that Thomas had had a skiing accident; he had been an expert skier.

She knew she had to get on with her life, but today it was difficult to see beyond the pain of loss.

The door opened suddenly, and Samuel Coleman's intrusion into her office demanded her full attention.

Sitting behind her desk, she drew in a deep, fortifying breath and forced the sad thoughts to the back of her mind. She would need all her strength to handle Samuel Coleman, the other executive vice-president of the bank. "Yes?"

"I have a few questions about your departmental budget for the upcoming fiscal year, Mrs. Dole. We need to discuss it now."

Silently counting to ten, Kate strove to keep the anger from her features as well as from her voice. "I'm afraid that's impossible, Mr. Coleman. You'll have to check with my secretary to see when I have some free time. I have a full schedule today. In fact, I have an appointment in five minutes.'' She checked her watch to emphasize the point.

''This needs to be ready for Robert's approval by the end of the week. Since it's your department in question, I think you'd better try to fit me in immediately.'' Resentment flared in his cool eyes, the line of his jaw harsh as he leaned into her desk, his hands spread wide on the wooden top.

This time she had to count to twenty. Ever since Kate had been promoted to head the lending division of the bank, Samuel's hostility had become more blatant. He had wanted to be in charge of Kate's division, but Robert Simon, president and owner of the bank, had decided that Samuel was doing too good a job as the head of the operation-and-administration division to move him.

''*I* don't have any questions about my department,'' Kate answered finally in a crisp tone. ''I couldn't possibly see you before tomorrow, Mr. Coleman.''

Their gazes clashed in a silent battle of willpower. Then, just as suddenly as he had entered, Samuel left.

Kate relaxed slowly, the tension easing. There were times like this, after an encounter with Samuel, when she felt like Humpty Dumpty and wondered if she would ever piece her life back together again.

Damn Samuel Coleman for making her feel as though she had to defend her position as executive vice-president. He thought she had got the job because Robert and her father were good friends. But Robert wouldn't have given her the job unless he had thought she would be an asset.

She had been in the loan department for twelve years and had quickly worked her way up through the managerial hierarchy because of her diligence and knowledge of finance. After her husband's death she had thrown herself into her job and worked twice as hard. She had become vice-president of the loan department, and when Morris Appleton left a few months before, she and the other two vice-presidents had been the logical candidates for Morris's position as executive vice-president. It hadn't been as easy as Samuel had implied, but she was thankful for her job because it had been a salvation after Thomas's death.

When her secretary announced over the intercom that Cade Weston had arrived for his appointment, Kate wasn't ready for the meeting. She needed to be alone to work through her feelings, but with her busy schedule that wouldn't be possible.

She was halfway across her office when the door opened and Cade Weston entered. For a brief second her step faltered, but she quickly mustered her businesslike poise and greeted him with a handshake.

The warm strength of his grip, coupled with a sense of bold recklessness, had Kate nonplussed. This man before her was tough, aggressive, individualistic, a man who would control his own destiny at all costs. She wasn't sure where the impression came from, but it was a sharp, clear one. Perhaps because she knew why he was here. Perhaps because she had met other men like him, all involved in exploring for oil, a risky business full of opportunities and full of disappointments. Cade Weston was sure to be the type of man who put everything he owned on the line on the chance one of his wells would strike black gold.

The lift of one dark brow brought a stop to her intense study of him. Slowly her smile of welcome came, and he responded with one of his own. The brackets at the corners of his mouth mitigated the rugged severity of his square jawline.

"I'm Cade Weston, Mrs. Dole. I wanted to see you about a line of credit."

His voice, rich and pleasant, was full of masculine amusement. Humor simmered in his probing regard and was quickly masked as she steadfastly matched his direct look.

"Please, have a seat, Mr. Weston." Kate indicated a chair in front of her desk before she moved behind it to sit down, pausing a moment to compose herself for the meeting. Normally she never reacted so strongly to a client, but then, the day was hardly normal. "How much of a line of credit are you applying for?"

"In the last nine years I've been successful in my overrides. I'm now earning six thousand dollars a month with them. I'd like to start with two hundred thousand dollars."

The quiet steel tone in his voice underlined the determination that Kate had glimpsed a few minutes before. "We'll need to see copies of the wells' production records, as well as credit references. I'll have our own reservoir engineer look into what he thinks these wells will be producing for the next five years."

While she listed what was needed, his expression held an intensity of purpose that she seldom encountered, making her feel as though she'd been given a reprieve. Now he shifted his incredible dark eyes, the color of the oil he sought, to the briefcase on his lap and opened it.

"I have everything you need right here." Cade placed the papers on her desk and slid them toward her.

She glanced through them before looking up. "Everything seems to be in order. What are you going to do with the money, Mr. Weston?"

"I want to purchase two land leases that I've lined up and start drilling on one as soon as possible."

"Is this all the collateral you have?"

"Yes, that's it—except for my pickup," he added with a sly smile, "which is paid for."

As she had expected, he was putting everything he had on the line. What made a person gamble like that? He had a healthy income from his work for Keyes Petroleum Corporation as their head geologist. He had the time to sit back and not rush into anything. But from his application she noticed that he had recently quit working for Howard Keyes and was already sinking all his money into an oil venture that could bankrupt him within six months. "I see, Mr. Weston."

"Do you?"

The question was spoken quietly, but Kate heard the skepticism. "Yes, I do. I've worked in this bank's lending department for a number of years and have seen many people risk everything to start their own businesses. Some make it. Others don't." *And it always bothers me when they don't,* she added silently.

Cade bent forward, his eyes locked with hers. "I'll be one of those who make it."

The iron discipline was in his voice again, and Kate couldn't help but respect someone who had so much faith in himself. *He's a loner,* she thought as she reviewed his application, needing to sever the visual, electric contact that had imprisoned her for a breathless moment.

"Mr. Weston, we will give due consideration to your request for a two-hundred-thousand-dollar line of credit. I'll get back to you shortly." With a supreme effort, she kept her concern to herself. She couldn't allow a client to think she was soft, but with Cade Weston's venture she realized how much of a risk he was taking. As a human being, she was worried about it. As a banker, she would make sure the bank was covered.

Kate stood and extended her hand. When his fingers wrapped around hers, she tried to ignore the tingling sensation. But it was difficult to disregard. She hastily pulled her hand away, momentarily dazed by her reaction.

"One of the parcels I discovered recently is up for renewal soon. It's prime land for drilling and I'd like to get it. I hope I'll hear soon."

"We'll get to it as soon as possible, Mr. Weston."

Cade ran his hand through his sandy hair, feathered back from his face in thick waves. Self-mockery glittered in his dark-brown eyes. "Sorry for my impatience. Now that I have my first package together, I'm eager to start work. I'll try not to call you every day." Picking up his briefcase, he grinned. "Besides, I'm not even sure I could get through to you. Your secretary is very protective. I think I gave her my life history before I got an appointment."

Kate didn't usually handle the interviews for most loans. That task was for the vice-presidents and loan officers under her. But occasionally she did it for a friend or a big depositor or, in this case, for Robert Simon.

Walking with him toward the door, she said, "I promise to get to it quickly, Mr. Weston."

At the door, he replied in a deep drawl, "That's all I can ask, Mrs. Dole."

Before he strode away, he flashed her a brief grin that accelerated her heartbeat. She watched him leave and was sure he could move with a quickness that would take a person by surprise, even though he was over six feet four inches tall and solidly built.

When Kate turned back toward her office, she felt as though the energy level in the room had been cut to half. She tried to review his loan application again, but it was useless. She couldn't get past his name, Cade Matthew Weston. It would take a long time for a woman to know him fully— if ever. Behind those perceptive eyes was a reserve, a closed look that warned people not to trespass. With her husband she had shared everything, often knowing what he was going to say before he spoke. Intuitively, she knew that wouldn't be true with Cade.

What kind of man was Cade Weston? There had to be a certain hunger in him, a certain daring to challenge fate. He had to be an optimistic person, tempered with a ruthless determination to make it.

Denver, Colorado, had been founded by men like Cade, men who'd had the pioneer spirit. They'd known what they wanted and had gone after it with a single-mindedness that often excluded everything else. Her grandfather had been one of those men. She wondered if Cade would obtain his dream and suddenly, vehemently, hoped he would.

It took a moment for Kate to realize that her intercom was buzzing. "Yes?"

"Lisa Masters is here to see you."

"Send her in, please," Kate replied, and knew immediately why her friend had stopped in to see her.

The minute Lisa stepped into her office she said, "I'm taking you to lunch and I won't let you talk me out of it. I know this is unexpected, but I didn't want you to be alone today."

"Alone?" Kate said with a forced laugh. "How can a person be alone here?"

Lisa eased into the same chair Cade had sat in. "You can be alone in a crowd of a thousand.

We've been friends for a long time, Kathleen Dole. I know what today is.''

"A heavy workday."

"You have to eat sometime. So why not now, before the restaurants get crowded?"

"Okay," Kate conceded because she really didn't want to be alone. "I know I won't have a moment's peace until I agree to lunch. I just need to make one quick call, then I'll be ready." Kate dialed an in-house number and said, "I'll leave the Weston file with my secretary, Carl. I want the report on the wells as soon as possible."

When Kate hung up, she glanced at Lisa, whose features had whitened. "Is something wrong?"

"No," Lisa replied quickly, and stood. "Let's go. I'm starved."

"Are you sure you're okay?"

"I'm fine. I came to take your mind off your problems, and what better way than eating at Miguel's?"

Kate wasn't convinced everything was fine with Lisa, but it wouldn't do her any good to pursue the subject. She couldn't imagine, though, why her friend had suddenly looked so disconcerted.

"Cade here." He shifted the receiver to his other ear and picked up a pencil. Even before she identified herself, he knew it was Kathleen Dole. Over the past few days it had been hard to forget her voice, crisp and clear like an autumn day in the Rockies.

"This is Kathleen Dole, Mr. Weston."

So formal, Cade thought with a chuckle.

"I need to see you about your loan as soon as possible."

Cade tensed, his right hand tightening around the receiver. "Is there a problem, Mrs. Dole?"

"Possibly. I want to discuss putting a stipulation on the loan."

"What kind?" A frown was carved deep into his features.

"Since it's after closing time, can you be here at four-thirty Monday afternoon?"

His temper flared. He didn't like his question being ignored, especially when it concerned his dream. A stipulation could constrict him, something he wanted to avoid if possible. "What kind of stipulation?" he asked in a voice full of authority.

"I'll see you at four-thirty on Monday, Mr. Weston. We'll discuss it then."

It took considerable willpower to say goodbye in a level voice. With his hand resting on the receiver, he thought seriously of calling Mrs. Kathleen Dole back and demanding to discuss the stipulation. But he had come to think of banks as conservative and reserved. He wondered if Kathleen was. In fact, he'd been wondering about that woman a lot lately.

She certainly had the cool beauty that went along with his image of a banker. Her brown hair had been brushed in a conservative, neck-length style, but the dress she'd worn had surprised him. He'd expected a tailored business suit, but instead she'd worn a navy-blue-and-red silk dress with a soft cowl neckline and a full skirt that only hinted at her generous curves.

It was her dark-blue eyes that had really thrown him off. Behind her cool, professional facade he had glimpsed a sadness that he suspected she wasn't even aware she exuded. He'd read about her husband's fatal accident. Both Kathleen and Thomas were from prominent Denver families, and their life together had often been written about in the newspapers, especially the tragedy.

Cade knew the pain she was going through, trying to put her life back together after her husband's death. He had been there. That day in her office he'd been drawn to the same lonely confusion he had felt eight years before, when Rachel had died. He found himself wanting to help Kathleen get through it.

Shoving back his desk chair, he rose to his feet and stretched. How in the world can I offer anyone help when my own life is in such a mess? Cade wondered as he left his house to pick up his son at the theater. Kathleen Dole would be dangerous to all his well-thought-out plans. She was a woman who would demand everything from a man.

As he looked up at the cloudless blue sky of a hot afternoon, he instantly thought of Kathleen's eyes. He should be angry with her for not going into any more detail over the phone about his loan application. He knew when he heard inflexibility in a person's voice. But he was finding it hard to be angry at her when he remembered the haunted look in her eyes.

Cade climbed into his red pickup truck and headed downtown. He was mentally going over a list of possible investors for his first oil prospect when he caught sight of a new Masters building being constructed. Judd Masters was everywhere in Denver, continually reminding Cade of where he came from. A frown slashed across his tanned face as he turned his full attention back to the road.

Bastard! The word that had tormented him as a child bombarded him now, and he clenched the steering wheel tighter. Why did it still have to hurt after all these years? As usual, there was no answer.

Logically he knew he would never be able to change it and he'd learned to live with the cold hard facts of his birth. Emotionally...

Damn! That's enough wallowing, Weston.

Cade wiped his mind clean of all thoughts except the black asphalt ribbon of road ahead. He had control over his life. He had control over his emotions. He would make it on his own.

Parking his truck in front of the old movie house where the community theater was, Cade purposefully turned his thoughts toward the fishing trip he and his son had planned for the weekend.

Inside, he slipped into a seat in the back row to wait until rehearsal was over. Matthew was helping his grandmother with the scenery and costumes. Onstage the director was going through a scene with the actors.

"Cade, I need to talk to you for a moment."

Cade squinted toward the shadowy figure of his mother. He had heard the strain beneath her words and noticed she was nervously playing with the pincushion on her wrist.

Ruth Weston sat in the seat next to Cade and began, "I haven't had a chance to talk to you in private since Judd's heart attack last month."

"Why the hell did you go to the hospital after all he did to you?" His question was savage.

She sighed. "It was because of all he and I shared that I went. But that's not what I want to talk to you about. Lisa knows you're her half brother."

"Oh, God."

Cade closed his eyes; the image of his half sister the last time he had seen her was sharply and clearly imprinted in his mind. If she had known the truth of their relationship then, she hadn't indicated it, and he'd wanted to shout it at her. There were times when he was tired of the secrets, the lies surrounding his birth. He'd had to pretend that he hadn't known who she was. By the time that meeting had been over, she probably had wished she would never see him again.

But then, the mention of Judd's name always brought out the worst in him. Innocently Lisa Masters had asked him to work for Judd, developing some oil prospects. Cade had refused a good deal and a lot of money. Lisa hadn't been able to understand and he hadn't been able to explain it to her. He wanted nothing to do with his father or his money.

"Who told her?" Cade asked, staring at the stage but not really seeing the actors on it.

"Judd. His heart attack made him reassess his life."

"For once I actually feel sorry for him. For years I wanted to tell her, but I never could. How do you tell your daughter she has a bastard brother who lives in the same town? But then, Judd probably didn't care how Lisa felt."

"He cares, Cade. And he cares what you think," Ruth whispered in a choked voice.

"Then he has the most unusual way of showing it." Cade leaned forward, his elbows resting on his thighs, his hands laced loosely together. He and his mother didn't see eye to eye on the subject of Judd Masters. She saw Judd through rose-colored glasses. He saw his father for what he really was.

"Where's Matthew, Mom?" Cade finally asked.

"He's backstage. I'll get him." Ruth rose, turned toward Cade and started to say something but decided not to. Instead, she walked down the aisle toward the stage, her dark hair coiled in a knot at her neck, her quiet beauty and dignity stated in every gesture and feature. She paused to speak to the director a moment, then continued on backstage.

Cade followed her with his eyes, his pulse rate quickening. Looking at his mother a person wouldn't be aware of the rough times she had gone through. But he knew; his tightly clasped hands underscored the impotent rage he felt. Damn Judd Masters!

His mother had never married because of Judd. Hell, she didn't even date much. She just worked and worked at her store, as though keeping busy would ease the agony of all those wasted years, yearning for the man she loved. Judd Masters didn't deserve that kind of devotion.

The darkness enveloped Cade as his thoughts went backward in time. He could no longer control the flood of memories. They swept into his mind as though they had occurred only the day before: the taunts he had received as a child; the parents who wouldn't allow him to play with their sons because Cade was illegitimate and somehow tainted or dirty; the nights he would wake up and stay up because he didn't want to dream; the times he had desperately needed a father to talk to, to do things with; and above all, the attempts at hiding his feelings from his mother, who had gone through enough misery and didn't need any more.

She had tried to be both mother and father, and he had wanted to protect her from gossip and from his father. Why had his father come into his life when he had finally rid himself of the need?

The night of his high-school graduation still made him break out in a cold sweat whenever he thought about it. After Cade's speech as valedictorian, Judd had spoiled the victorious moment by going over to congratulate him. Cade didn't want anything from Judd Masters—not his money, not his congratulations, not his belated love and certainly not his interference.

It hadn't taken him long to realize that Judd didn't admit defeat and for some reason Judd had wanted to be included in his life after eighteen years of completely staying away. By setting up a trust fund, Judd had thought his money would buy his son's affection, but all Cade had ever wanted from his father had been his time and love. The smashing of his fist into the open palm of his hand shot pain up his arm and instantly sobered Cade.

The lights in the auditorium were on and the rehearsal was over. Matthew stood in front of him with a worried expression on his face.

"Dad, is something wrong?"

The fast beating of Cade's heart slowed as he focused his attention upon his twelve-year-old son. Judd could have had so much if only he'd wanted it. There had been a lot of love inside of Cade that had slowly been destroyed with each passing year of rejection.

Forcing a smile to his lips, Cade stood and laid both hands on Matthew's shoulders. "I love you, son. I want you to know that no matter what happens I'll always love you, no conditions attached."

"I know, Dad." Matthew threw his arms around his father and hugged him. Then, as though caught doing something "big" boys didn't do, Matthew quickly straightened and said, "I'm ready to go."

"Grandma doesn't need you anymore?"

"Nope. She's discussing something with Mr. Carson, the director."

"Well, then, let's go. We've got to pack the truck and get on the road. Those fish are just waiting to leap into our frying pan." He placed his arm around his son as they walked from the theater.

I don't commit easily, Cade thought, *but when I do, I don't turn my back on that person.* Love was an emotion he couldn't afford to throw around. It was an emotion that had brought him a lot of pain as a child and he vowed Matthew would never experience that kind of anguish.

Chapter Two

It was fifteen minutes after four. Cade would be here soon. Kate abandoned any pretense of working and walked to the window. The downtown traffic was becoming thick as the rush hour neared.

Distracted, Kate trailed her hand up and down the heavy material of the drape. Since their conversation on Friday, she had been on edge, finding herself prowling about or daydreaming rather than working.

The tenacious quality she had sensed in Cade at their first meeting had been very apparent during that brief phone conversation. He wasn't going to like what she had to say and now she wished she had handled it over the phone with miles of wire as their only connection. That had been her intention when she had first called him. But when she had heard his deep baritone voice, she had suddenly changed her mind. They would discuss this face-to-face. Cade deserved that much.

Cade Weston's intriguing, she decided, remembering the strength he exhibited that was tempered with an underlying gentleness. Crossing her office to pick up the folder on his loan application, Kate flipped through the information until she found what she was looking for. He had been married to Rachel Hawke, who had died eight years before, and he had a son named Matthew.

He would know what she was going through, trying to get on with her life after Thomas's death. He had gone down the same path.

As she sat down behind her desk, Kate wondered if that was what drew her toward Cade. Or was it the fact that he held himself apart from others? She had always been open and direct with the people around her. She had nothing to hide. She was there for people to like or not like; she held nothing in reserve. But Cade held everything in reserve, hidden in a tightly sealed box from the world. And she wanted to know why. She'd been wondering about it all weekend. A person didn't lock out the world without a reason—a good reason.

When her secretary buzzed to announce Cade, Kate was still not totally prepared for their meeting. She was constantly being sidetracked from the issue at hand. One part of her was telling her to let him handle the line of credit any way he saw fit, but the other part was cautioning her to protect the bank's interest at all costs. Cade would have something to say about the proposed stipulation.

Crossing her office, Kate smoothed her suit skirt into place, paused for a few seconds, then opened the door and stepped into the reception area. Smiling, she extended her hand toward Cade.

He shook her hand once, then quickly released it. There was absolutely no expression on his face; his dark-brown eyes were void of emotion. Kate felt chilled.

"Please step into my office," she said in a cool tone, gesturing toward the door. Then, when she was again seated behind her desk, she waited a full minute, feigning a study of the loan application she knew by heart. Finally Kate looked up into that blank expression and said, "I've reviewed the application and want to put in a stipulation that the money be used only for drilling."

No sound came to shatter the strained silence in her office. For a static moment she found herself rigid, waiting for his reaction. *Oh, he's good.* Not a flicker of emotion passed over his face.

"Why?" Cade asked finally.

"I have to have guarantees that you're a going concern. We're only interested in a company with a continual life. Do you have any acreage in inventory?"

"No. I told you I need the money not only for drilling but for buying the land leases. I have two lined up." There was only a slight edge to his voice.

"But none signed?"

"No." Alert, he leaned forward, his eyes glinting with a metallic sheen that impaled her. His casual air belied the trace of anger in his gaze. "I have to be able to use the money for both drilling and buying leases. My collateral is excellent. I assure you I have no intention of failing."

"People who ask for loans never do," Kate replied automatically, but somehow she thought the power and conviction behind his words were stronger than most. "Mr. Weston, I will propose a compromise. The bank will set a limit on how much can be used for buying land leases."

"How much?" His tone held an authoritative edge that defied resistance. He had entered her office prepared to fight for everything he needed.

Infuriated, Kate allowed the silence to lengthen before answering, "Forty thousand."

"I need fifty and then I can buy all the acreage I need for one of the leases." He reclined in the chair, diffusing the charged atmosphere, his male grace seemingly nonchalant.

"Agreed. Fifty it is." Kate jotted down the figure and made a few notes to review with the loan committee. "Of course, this will all depend on the reservoir engineer's report about your wells' projected production rates for the next five years."

Cade relaxed completely. "He'll find those wells solid bets. The bank won't lose any money on this deal."

No, the bank wouldn't lose. Kate would see that the bank's interests were protected. But what about Cade's? He could lose everything.

"We should have an answer for you in a week, Mr. Weston."

A roguish grin dented the arrogant slope of his mouth, dissolving any remnants of her anger. "Would you consider it a bribe if I asked you to join me for dinner?"

"Possibly, but I must warn you I'm too dedicated to my job for bribery to work."

"I'm a person who likes to find out things the hard way. I want an opportunity to convince you that I'm a good, solid risk."

"But a risk nevertheless," Kate retorted, though humor touched her voice and eyes.

"In order to make money, you have to be willing to risk money," Cade countered quickly.

"If you give me a few minutes, I need to wrap up a couple of things before I leave."

Rising to his feet in one smooth movement, Cade said, "I need to get my truck from the parking lot. I'll pick you up in front of the building in fifteen minutes."

"Fine." Kate started to stand but Cade waved her back down.

"I can find my own way out." His eyes sparkled with mischief, the tension of moments before totally gone in that one carefree look.

For the first two minutes after he left, Kate just stared at the door that he had closed behind him. With her fingers entwined and her elbows resting on her desk, she tried to bring order to her chaotic thoughts. She was probably reading too much into his surprise dinner invitation, but she had all but told him outright that he would get the loan if everything checked out. He didn't have to "bribe" her.

She wanted this dinner to be purely social; she had made a promise to herself to get on with her life, and tonight was the beginning. No business, she decided as she quickly took care of some small details.

Kate was outside the Simon building as Cade pulled his truck up to the curb and hopped out to open the door.

"Punctual on top of everything else," Cade commented once he was back in the cab and removing his suit jacket. He pulled his truck out into the stream of heavy traffic heading out of the downtown area.

"To a banker it's unforgivable to be late."

"How about a smile? Is that forbidden?"

Puzzled, Kate whispered, "Smile?"

"Since I picked you up a few minutes ago, your face has been the picture of perfect somberness. This is after-hours." While stopped at a light, he slanted her a tender grin. "No business tonight?"

His look was pure seduction. The sudden intimacy in the truck was warm and gentle like a brief summer shower.

As the truck moved forward, Kate answered in a breathless voice, "None."

"Good. This last month has been especially long, and tonight all I want to do is relax and enjoy a good meal—" he paused only a few seconds, but long enough for Kate to see an almost elusive yearning in his expression before he added "—in the company of someone interesting."

Kate gave a short laugh, compressing her lips into a false frown. "I think that last was thrown in to keep your banker appeased and happy."

He tossed a quick, speculative glance at her. "I never say something unless I really mean it—Kate."

"How did you know I go by the name of Kate, rather than Kathleen, Kathy, Kit . . ."

He silenced her recital of names with his low rippling laughter that rang from deep within his chest. "Easy. We know some of the same people. We'd never been formally introduced until our meeting at the bank, but, lady, I know who you are."

The intimacy heightened, and Kate was thankful it was rush hour. Cade had to concentrate totally on the traffic, giving her time to gather her thoughts. She watched him drive, his long supple fingers grasping the steering wheel, his sharp gaze alert in the mad traffic, the sinewy muscles of his arms exposed beneath his short-sleeve shirt.

He wore a tan suit that fit well and looked good on him, but Kate sensed he was more comfortable wearing blue jeans out in an oil field. He was more rugged than handsome, she decided as her gaze lowered, taking in his long length.

When she leisurely returned her regard to his face, her breathing was arrested for a few seconds by his penetrating look, which cracked her composure completely. They were again stopped in a line of cars, but she hadn't even noticed.

His eyes told her nothing until they boldly inventoried her assets, much like a banker would when considering a loan. His almost-black eyes missed not one feature as they traveled from her hair to her toes, then back up to her face. An intensity burned in the dark depths of his gaze as it locked with hers.

An eternity passed.

The blaring of a horn behind them severed the invisible link. The explosive desire she had felt for him in that moment had been reflected in his eyes. Unnerved by feelings she hadn't experienced in a long time, Kate stared straight ahead. Glancing sideways, she saw the whitened grip he had on the steering wheel and knew he was as affected as she was.

Kate laughed shakily as Cade pulled into a restaurant's parking lot. An old oil derrick had been erected in the front of the restaurant. "You're never far away from it, are you?"

His grin was sheepish when it came. "Nope. The food is excellent and the atmosphere..."

"Inspiring?"

"Familiar might be a better word," he said as he touched her waist casually to guide her toward the Black Gold's front entrance.

"I can see what you mean," Kate commented as they passed the old derrick.

"That's a cable-tool rig," Cade explained when Kate stopped to inspect it. "They're rarely seen anymore. At one time that was what was used. Now, though, we use a rotary-drilling rig."

Inside, the lighting was dim and the oil theme was continued. There were outdated gas pumps and old gas-station symbols and signs, and on the walls hung brown-tinted photographs of oil fields, gushing wells and famous oilmen.

After they were shown to a booth, Cade sat across from Kate and ordered a beer. Kate shook her head when he asked if she wanted one, too. For a moment she studied the old photographs on the wooden-planked wall next to her. She became caught up in reading an article about J. Paul Getty, who had made his first million in the oil industry.

Suddenly a thought hit her: how could she forget something as important as her car? She laughed.

"Is it a secret or can you share it with a curious guy?"

"I left my car in the downtown garage where I park. I should have followed you here. I don't know what I was thinking. I normally..."

Suddenly she didn't know how to explain her out-of-character behavior to the man who had caused it. She was always so organized that it was hard for her to understand it herself.

The hand that had been reaching for her water glass dropped to the table. His steadfast look seared through to her soul. A message as complex and compelling as the man was communicated in the powerful ardor of his gaze. When his hand covered hers on the table, his thumb rubbed a gentle circle over her wrist.

"After dinner I'll take you to get your car."

The soft touch of his hand wiped her mind blank, and it took a moment for her to answer.

"No, that's okay. I can call my secretary and ask her to pick me up tomorrow morning. It's on her way."

"Are you sure?"

No, I'm not sure of anything when you're around, she silently answered him, but aloud said, "Yes. I don't live far from here. Going downtown again is out of the way for both of us."

Kate watched the dim lights of the restaurant play over his features, creating shadows, illusions. His thumb continued its lazy assault. The sounds of the restaurant faded, and her world narrowed to the feel of his skin against hers, to the male scent that lightly teased her, to the melting depths of his eyes.

If their waiter hadn't arrived with Cade's beer and the menus, Kate realized she could have sat there all night staring into his fathomless eyes, trying to figure out the man behind them. She had always been fascinated by a good mystery.

When Cade's hand left hers, she felt abandoned and wished she had the right to recapture it. Instead, she took her own menu from the waiter and tried to concentrate on food. Her stomach knotted with frustration.

Kate laughed a bit nervously. "Even the menu is oil related. Roughneck Saturday Night On The Town. Tool Pusher's Gusher. The Driller's Pay Dirt. I think I'll be daring and try a Roustabout T-bone. What's a roustabout?"

"He helps the foreman on an oil well," Cade answered, a hint of stiffness in his voice. In the restaurant's intimate setting this spontaneous dinner had turned into something more—something he wasn't sure should continue. She had implied that he would get the loan, and he had wanted to celebrate and share the victory with her. But now he knew he had been lying to himself, that his reasons for the dinner invitation went beyond that. He was confused by the powerful attraction between them.

After they placed their orders, Cade asked in a voice that was totally neutral, "How's your brother's campaign coming along?"

A safe subject, she thought. "He's just started getting his organization together. It's going to take a lot of hard work to defeat the incumbent congressman."

Throughout the rest of the dinner, they discussed "safe" subjects, and Cade's expression remained as aloof as a lone oil derrick on a vast stretch of flatland with nothing around for miles.

When they had finished dinner, Cade paid the check, then stood, assisting Kate from the booth. But this time Cade didn't place his hand at her waist to guide her. He walked a good foot away from her, as though not just mentally but physically establishing a barrier between them.

On the ride to her house Kate kept telling herself it was for the best that nothing had happened. She wasn't sure she was ready to handle the feelings that would exist if she allowed herself to give in to them. She had married Thomas while in college and had been married most of her adult life. It had been a comfortable, open relationship with no big highs or lows. With Cade Weston that wouldn't be the case.

At a stoplight, Cade drummed his fingers on the steering wheel and cursed himself for asking Kate out to dinner. What in the hell had he been thinking? A casual affair wasn't for a woman like Kate. And a casual affair was all he had to offer.

When he parked the truck outside her house, she asked out of politeness, "Would you like to come in for some coffee? Or a drink?"

Dangerous. Not wise. Tempting. Cade twisted around to face her, his arm resting along the back of the seat. "No, I'd better not. I still have some work to do."

Half relieved, half disappointed, she reached for the door handle. "I understand."

Cade touched her hand, the contact of his fingers on her skin as hot and devastating as the vibrant colors of the sunset that scored the horizon.

"Do you understand, Kate?"

She pulled her hand away from his touch. "Yes, I think I do. We're both confused by what's happening between us. Why did you ask me out?"

Her blunt question nonplussed him for a brief moment. Like the woman, Cade thought. "You're certainly direct."

"I see no reason to be any other way. Game playing bores me. It's a waste of time."

"I don't play games, Kate. I asked you out because I wanted to. Why did you come?"

"I'm not sure," she answered slowly, then stopped, drew in a deep breath and continued, "Yes, I am. You interest me."

Cade whistled, not used to a woman who spoke her mind so candidly. "The timing is all wrong for us."

"I didn't know there was an 'us.'"

Cade trailed the back of his hand down her jawline. "We both know there could be," he replied in a smoky voice, his hand sliding behind her neck and into the rich thickness of her hair.

Slowly, he pulled her toward him. He gave her the time to move away, but he hoped she wouldn't. Before he walked away from her, he wanted to kiss her once. Maybe that would be all he'd have to do to end her disquieting image in his thoughts.

His mouth moved gently against hers. When she offered no resistance, he increased the pressure of his lips, his tongue rubbing back and forth over her closed mouth, enticing it to open. She parted her lips slightly, as if they were a bud opening up to welcomed sunlight. The kiss deepened.

Cade gathered her close to him, savoring the smooth interior of her mouth, the tactile feel of her softness. He wanted to reach inside and become a part of her. He knew if he was going to stop he had to do it now. He didn't want to.

As Cade started to deepen the kiss even more, she wedged her hands between them and pushed away. "No," she whispered. "You're right about the timing being all wrong. I can't handle a roller-coaster ride. I'm just getting everything put back together."

He didn't look at her as she left his truck. He couldn't. He had told her he didn't play games, but wasn't that what he'd just done? He wasn't particularly pleased with himself at the moment.

"Damn! What a mess," he muttered as he backed out of her driveway. He was attracted to Kate Dole. He liked her and this was the worst possible time for them.

Life was not simple and there were just some things a person could not have, Cade decided as he drove home.

Once inside, Cade fixed himself a whiskey and water. He was sipping it when the phone rang. He snatched up the receiver, half wishing it was Kate.

"Cade, this is Judd."

Cade downed the rest of his drink. Somehow he had known Judd would call.

"I heard from Howard that you've decided to start your own oil company."

Judd always knew what Cade was doing. *Sometimes before I know myself,* Cade thought bitterly.

"Are you?" Judd's voice took on an impatience.

Cade's persistent silence always annoyed Judd more than when he did speak. That was a lesson he'd learned well from the master himself. When he was a teenager and ranted and raved for his father to leave him alone, that he didn't want his trust fund for college, Judd had always met his anger with a lethal silence that made Cade feel very young and foolish afterward.

"Do I really need to answer? You seem to know everything," Cade finally replied sarcastically.

"Where are you going to get the money to start this company?" Judd demanded.

Cade could tell by Judd's terse voice that he had hit a nerve. Cade started to tell his father to mind his own business, but before he could say anything, he remembered Judd's recent heart attack. Cade reached for the whiskey bottle and poured some more into his glass. It wouldn't make any difference if his father knew; Judd would find out soon anyway. He always did.

"The usual place. At a bank." Cade's movements were jerky as he brought the glass to his lips and finished his drink in two swallows.

"The Denver Exchange Bank."

"Did you read that in your crystal ball?" Cade slammed the glass down on the table so hard it cracked. He retreated into silence.

There was a lengthy pause before Judd said, "I know Robert Simon."

People might not know about their connection, but Judd had his ways of keeping tabs on his life. Cade felt caged, controlled by his father despite his efforts not to be. It seemed the harder he fought Judd, the more determined Judd became. Cade's jaw clamped down; his features were hard and cynical. "Is there anyone you don't use?"

There was another long pause before Judd admitted, "Very few. But my life history isn't why I called. There's no need for you to go to a bank, Cade. We can work out a deal between us."

Cade's anger held him rigid. He was afraid to answer for fear of exploding. He had to keep a rein on his temper. He wouldn't give Judd the satisfaction of knowing he had aroused his anger.

"There's nothing between us except a biological accident."

"Your trust fund is still there."

"I told you I won't accept a penny from you. I meant it then and I mean it now. You worked hard to get your money and you're welcome to every last cent of it."

Tension crackled over the line.

"You're quick to condemn without knowing all the facts, Cade."

"I know all I need to know. Ruth was pregnant with your child when you married your wife. Was Anne's money that attractive?" With all the restraint he could muster, Cade quietly replaced the receiver on its hook.

His hand shook as he lifted the cracked glass from the counter. Anger, hurt and frustration battered at him like a drill bit eating away inch by inch at the earth's crust, constant and forceful.

The phone rang again and Cade snapped around to stare at the instrument. "Control someone else, Judd! You can't have me!"

The phone ringing was wearing him down as Judd meant it to, and Cade quaked with rage. "Damn you to hell!"

The glass went sailing through the air and smashed against the wall, sharp fragments flying everywhere. Immobilized, Cade was oblivious to the shards of glass around his feet. The jarring ring of the phone pierced his anger-numbed mind, bringing with it childhood memories.

He clenched and unclenched his hands, trying to halt the stream of turbulent thoughts, the pain of remembering the total rejection, the need for his father's love. He desperately fought within himself to claim the tough self-restraint that he had over his emotions. Hate and love were intense, ravaging emotions that took a person's control away from him. They were useless to him. Yet, Judd always managed to get to him.

The phone stopped ringing. The shattered glass mirrored his own feelings: splintered, strewn everywhere in hundreds of different pieces as if a savage storm had gotten hold of them. Cade retreated farther within himself, appalled at feeling anything toward Judd, even hate.

Chapter Three

Stay calm. But the thought did nothing to cool Kate's escalating temper.

She sat so straight in her chair that she wondered if she would snap in two like a tree during a tornado. Her look, aimed at Samuel Coleman, would have made anyone pause before speaking. But Samuel was furious and beyond caring.

"Leave the folder and I'll see what I can do to fix the error," Kate managed to say in a level voice while she seethed inside.

"See that this doesn't happen again. This might not be your mistake, but you are responsible for everyone under you." Samuel slammed the folder down on her desk.

"You don't have to tell me what I'm responsible for. The error will be amended and the new information on your desk Monday. I'll see to it personally."

Samuel glared at her for a few more seconds before turning abruptly and heading for the door. These confrontations always left her shaken, and Cade would be here any moment to sign the loan papers.

It had been eleven days since their last meeting, and Kate hadn't stopped thinking about him. She wouldn't pretend to herself that she didn't want to see Cade again. Trying to ignore the attraction she felt toward him wouldn't solve anything; she knew she risked being hurt deeply because with a man like Cade everything was so intense.

Her secretary announced Cade's arrival, and Kate quickly crossed her office. This time there was no hesitation because she had only good news for Cade.

Kate greeted Cade with a wide smile, extending her hand. His fingers closed around hers, not really shaking her hand but squeezing it gently. She enjoyed the warmth and roughness of his hand around hers. His smile was utterly engaging with a hint of masculine interest in it; her heartbeat responded by quickening its pace.

Slowly it dawned on her that they were still standing in her outer office with her secretary seated not three feet away. She cleared her throat, withdrew her hand from his and said, "I have everything ready for you to sign."

Even to herself her voice sounded strange. With amused patience, he waited for her to enter her office first, his look gauging her. Kate felt more in control when she was seated behind her desk, glancing over the papers before sliding them across to Cade. She watched as he carefully read the documents and a frown deepened the lines on his face.

"Where's the stipulation?" He glanced up; his jaw twitched, his body tensed, but both reactions were fleeting and quickly camouflaged.

"We decided to drop it."

"We?"

"Robert Simon." She had been puzzled by the president's interference in a normal routine loan, but then, she had met with Cade in the first place because Robert had asked her to handle it personally.

The hard line of his jaw clenched into a fierce expression. "Why?"

"He felt the bank was covered adequately without it."

For a brief moment Cade contemplated turning the loan down because he knew Judd was behind all this. But he wasn't a fool; he might not like it, but he would take the loan under any terms. The bottom line was he had to have it, and Judd had known that.

Cade placed the papers on the desk, careful to conceal his anger directed toward Judd. "Where do I sign?"

They stared at each other, and Kate wished they weren't in her office but somewhere romantic, sharing a quiet dinner and intimate conversation.

Leaning forward slightly, she indicated the lines where Cade should sign, her eyes sweeping upward from the papers to be trapped within his fervent regard again. Everything within her stopped: her heartbeat, her breathing, her common sense. The only thing that occupied her thoughts was the sheer masculine impact of Cade Weston.

The bewitching moment was destroyed when Cade terminated the visual contact. She watched his long, lean fingers grasp a pen, curling around it as he scrawled his name on the various lines needed. She wondered what those fingers would feel like tangled in her hair, curling around her arm, caressing her body; she wrenched her gaze away to stare out the window.

Cade was definitely all male. It showed in his eyes, his confident manner, his body. His raw sensuality only heightened her excitement. She wondered what he would be like completely out of control, like a well that had hit an unexpected gas pocket and had blown, and knew she wanted to find out.

Kate brought her attention back to him as he finished with the loan papers. A smile cracked his neutral expression, his mouth bracketed by deep creases.

"I feel like I just signed my life away."

"You did," Kate replied in a serious voice. For some reason she felt she had a personal stake in his success or failure. He might not be concerned about himself, but she was.

"This is only a means to an end. The first step toward a goal."

His statement was casual, but underneath she heard the barest trace of apprehension. "I'd love to treat you to a drink to celebrate that first step." Kate fleetingly thought she should be embarrassed for asking him out, but ever since he had walked into her office, she had wanted to.

His eyes took on a deep, liquid look, but instantly his black lashes drifted partially down to conceal his expression from her. "I'm sorry, Kate, but I have to pick up my son in thirty minutes. I'll have to take a rain check."

"Yes, of course."

As Kate escorted Cade to the door, she wondered if he was just being polite. She hoped he would call, but there was no way to tell with Cade.

Stepping into the reception area, Cade turned to say goodbye, wishing he had been free to accept her invitation. He wasn't sure what to say to her and was glad that Robert Simon appeared to say hello. As Cade greeted Robert, he noticed the pallor beneath the older man's dark complexion. Too much sitting behind a desk, Cade thought. That was what he liked the most about his job: the fieldwork, being at the rig, seeing all those hours studying the various maps bearing fruit.

Robert nodded his head toward Kate before speaking to Cade. "Last week Howard told me you were working on an oil prospect. I've been looking for some investments and I'd be interested when you have everything in order. Howard has a lot of faith in you as a geologist. Says you have a nose for oil."

Cade laughed. "I sure hope so."

Kate's earlier agreement about everything being placed on the line only underscored Cade's own feelings. But instead of being as scared as he probably should be, he was excited. It was the first real step toward a dream he'd had since college.

"I'll be closing the deal on the land next week and I can get back to you after that, Robert." He had something to prove to the banker: that he could make it without Judd's help.

"How deep do you think you'll have to drill the first well?" Robert asked as he started walking Cade toward the elevators.

Cade tossed a last glance at Kate, who still stood in the reception area. His look told her what he couldn't say moments before. *I am interested.* Then he turned back to answer Robert.

At the elevator Cade and Robert shook hands before Cade stepped through the open doors. As they swished closed, he glimpsed Kate in the background, watching him leave.

Okay, Weston, you're interested and she's interested. What are you going to do about it?

Nothing, if I'm smart.

Who said you were smart?

"I'm so glad you could come, Cade," Kate said, her blue eyes as clear as the beautiful July day.

"A free meal and good company is hard to turn down."

"Company you will definitely have." Kate laughed as she swept out her arm at the people milling about the lawn of her parents' home. "Every year Dad and Mom have an open house on the Fourth to repay some of their social debts."

"Not a bad idea. For a senator the Fourth is the most appropriate holiday. I suppose Greg will be here, following in his father's footsteps."

They passed between two groups of people and Cade moved closer, taking her arm. Kate hoped he wouldn't release his hold, but he did as soon as they stood under the tent where the buffet table was set up.

"Yes, but not until later. He had to attend a political rally, but he couldn't pass this up, either. When you start campaigning, you find yourself being run ragged. I'm glad it's my brother and not me running for Congress."

"I don't envy your brother, either, Kate, but I do understand why he does it. There's as much excitement in the political arena as there is exploring for oil. I doubt politics is dull."

"And drilling for oil isn't dull, either? Is that why you do it?"

"Partly, yes. Drilling for oil and bringing in a well is exhilarating. There isn't any way I can really describe the high you're on when you strike oil. It's a thrilling challenge to guess where to drill and when that well comes in . . ." Cade could not find the words to finish explaining.

Kate turned toward Cade. "Did you get the land lease you wanted?" She was interested in everything he was doing, and that interest had nothing to do with the loan. It was purely personal. It had taken her a while to accept that, but when she acknowledged that the attraction she felt for Cade wouldn't go away, she had asked him to this party.

"A few days ago. I can just smell the oil below ground." His voice wasn't much faster than a drawl and had a deliciously sexy rasp to it.

Kate laughed. "You sound like one of those old-timers from the early days of the oil boom who swore they could sniff out oil from fifty feet."

"They were probably right. Oil was much easier to get to in those days." Cade looked beyond Kate, a faraway expression in his eyes as he continued, "There's something about using all your years of knowledge, poring over the sand maps, appraising the rock formations and then having to take a calculated guess. You never know for sure until the day your drill bit cuts through and releases that black gold and it surges up after being locked inside the earth for millions of years. Everything's worth it when that day happens."

If that day comes, Kate thought, and wished she could do more to help his dream come true.

Cade looked back down at Kate, a lopsided grin on his face. "I think we should avoid the subject of oil or you may never shut me up."

"Sir, you can talk all you want. It certainly isn't something I can accuse you of doing a lot of."

"Kate, your mother wants you to meet some people we know from Washington before they leave," her father said as he joined them. "I'll keep this young man entertained until you get back. I take it you're Cade Weston?"

"Yes, sir."

"I'll be just a minute," Kate said as she quickly headed toward her mother and the couple, not wanting to be away from Cade for even a few minutes. *Possessive, aren't you,* she thought with a wry twist to her mouth.

Cade followed Kate's progress across the lawn with his eyes, then, remembering her father, returned his attention to Walter Stanfield. Kate's father commanded a lot of respect in Colorado and Washington. His reputation of being a tough but fair senator had earned him the admiration of the press, and Cade found himself very relaxed with the man.

"Kate tells me you used to work for Howard Keyes until you decided to start your own business, Cade. Have you put together your first package yet?"

"I'm working it up for prospective investors to look at." Cade saw a lot of Walter in Kate. They had the same dark hair, sharp, clear blue eyes and direct, open attitude.

"Where's your land lease?"

"In eastern Colorado."

"When you put it together, come see me. I'm always searching for a good investment." Walter looked beyond him to Kate, who was making her way back. His smile, directed at his daughter, was deep and loving as he clasped Kate's hand. "How in the world did you manage to get away from the Martins so quickly?"

"I guess I'm just lucky, Dad." She gazed at Cade through lowered lashes, hoping her feelings weren't written all over her face. She had practically been rude to the Martins, which had shocked her mother, when they kept talking and talking about silly, unimportant matters. The only thing that concerned her was Cade and getting to know him better. It was almost impossible with so many people around, but she had been encouraged when he'd discussed his oil lease.

"Ah, I see Greg has finally arrived. I'm going to have to have a talk with that son of mine. He's working way too hard. If he doesn't slow down he won't have anything left after he wins." Walter squeezed her hand briefly before walking away to join Kate's brother.

"Dad has never quite accepted the fact that Greg wanted to go into politics. He doesn't say anything to my brother about it now, but they used to have terrible arguments." Kate shivered, remembering one particular argument right before Greg had announced his intentions.

"Do all fathers try to dictate what their sons will do?"

The savagery in Cade's voice took Kate by surprise. Puzzled, she answered, "My father doesn't want Greg's life to be continually onstage the way his has been. My older brother is a very private person, and Dad feels the life of a congressman will be hard on him even though he believes Greg will make a good legislator. But my brother made his decision to take the bad with the good."

"Taking one day at a time?" Cade's eyes darkened to a pitch-black and his singeing regard raked her features boldly.

The intensity in Cade's eyes affected her as no one's ever had in the past. "Yes," she answered in a whisper. "Who can predict what tomorrow will bring? Life is a risk with no guarantees, like drilling for oil."

His eyes went blank. "I believe in taking one day at a time, but I also believe in planning and dreaming."

Yes, he would have to be a dreamer to do what he does, Kate thought.

"And there are things you can do to minimize your risks, Kate."

Suddenly they were no longer talking about the risks involved in drilling for oil. "You have to put emotions in to get any in return, Cade."

"Emotions aren't endless. There comes a time when you draw on them and there's nothing there."

Her mouth stretched into a smile that really wasn't felt. Her concern for Cade was strong because something was eating at him, preventing him from feeling completely. She wanted to be the one to change that. She wanted to make him feel whole again. That realization took her by surprise because she wasn't sure she had the ability.

Kate heard the sounds of laughter, of people talking, but the only thing she was really aware of was the rapid rise and fall of her chest, the liquid brown depths of Cade's eyes and the feverish heat of her body.

Someone bumped into her, and Cade reached out to steady her. She gazed down at his fingers, rough but gentle, encircling her arm, then looked up at him. A strong sensual tether instantly linked them together before she lowered her lashes to hide the desire she felt.

"I'm starved," Kate said weakly. She was disconcerted; she fought to strengthen her voice as she explained, "I forgot to eat breakfast this morning and I didn't take the time for lunch." Finally the lightness she wanted to project was injected into her voice.

Cade glanced at his watch. "It's nearly five."

"You're kidding." Kate, unconscious of what she was doing, grasped his wrist and examined his watch. Then it hit her that she was touching Cade and that it was hard to think coherently while doing it. Slowly her head came up, her eyes embracing his. "I can't believe..."

His skin was hotter than hundred-degree weather. His look was undermining her self-control. She had been wrong to think that the day was nice for a lawn party. It was hot!

"Kate, I..." The heightened sensuality that pulsated between them stole the last of his sentence. He finally continued in a raspy voice, "I'm glad you asked me to this open house. I hadn't planned anything special for the Fourth. Matthew went camping with some friends."

Leaving him alone. She had to remind herself that Cade was a survivor. Men like him were unconquerable, like the raw West with its deserts and mountains. But she couldn't ignore the sadness she heard in his voice. The Fourth was a time for family, but this year he was alone and didn't want to be. And she was alone and didn't want to be.

She released her grasp on his wrist and raised her hand to his jaw, feeling the cleanly shaven skin beneath her fingertips. Astonished at her own boldness, Kate pulled away, as though his jaw had been acid, eating away at her fingertips.

They continued to stare at each other wordlessly.

"Kate, I've already said goodbye to your mother and father and I just wanted to tell you how much Martha and I enjoyed the party this year."

Robert Simon and his wife stood beside them, commanding Kate's attention when all she wanted was to escape with Cade. Duty was the farthest thing from her mind, but the mocking gleam in Cade's eyes reminded her of it. Reluctantly she turned to the Simons and smiled.

"Are you two leaving already?" Kate asked politely.

"Yes, we have another party to go to." Robert turned toward Cade and added, "I'd like to meet with you sometime at the end of next week. My schedule is full until Thursday."

"I'll call your secretary and set up an appointment." The references to business dulled the playful glint in Cade's eyes.

"Good. I imagine you want to start drilling as soon as possible. Good day, Kate, Cade." Robert nodded to both of them as he and his wife walked away.

Before Kate had a chance to turn back to Cade, he was guiding her toward the buffet table. Grinning, he winked at her, devilment in his eyes. "I don't want you to faint from lack of food, and if too many more people interrupt us we'll never make it to the table."

"I'm in your capable hands, sir." The second Kate spoke the teasing sentence, she blushed.

The playfulness in his eyes was transformed into pure desire. "I believe I'd like that."

His reply, drawled close to her ear, was spiced with humor. His breath on its shell ignited hot flames within her, and her pulse pounded out of control.

Without another word, they filled their plates with smoked turkey and ham, cheese, sliced fruit and the freshly baked biscuits that were Kate's contribution to the mounds of dishes sitting on the long, white-clothed table.

When they were seated at a table under the tent that had been set up, Cade studied his plate for a moment, then arched one thick brow and asked, "Where's the hot dogs and apple pie?"

Kate's laughter filled the space between them as she waved toward one end of the long table. "They're there, we just didn't get that far. What's a Fourth of July celebration without the traditional American food?"

"You had me worried for a moment." His eyes shone like newly polished ebony.

Kate's stomach rumbled with hunger, destroying the delicately honed tension that had held her as his gaze caressed each feature with his own craving. She bent her head and attacked the food on her plate.

Moments later Cade chuckled. "You *were* starved."

She brought her head up. "I never lie."

"I know," was his quiet reply. "That's one of the things I like about you. Your candor."

She was lost in the swirling depths of his eyes. *Oh, Lord, he's overwhelming.* She shifted her gaze to the crowd in the tent, trying to divert her attention from the desire mounting within her.

"Lisa! You came after all." Kate jumped to her feet when she saw her friend.

Lisa Masters turned at the sound of Kate's voice. Lisa smiled, but the smile quivered, then disappeared entirely when she looked from her friend to Cade.

"I was looking for you. Your father told me you were in the tent." Lisa had spoken to Kate, but her gaze was on Cade.

Apprehension constricted Cade's chest as though someone were pulling a rawhide strap tightly around him. Lisa knew he was her half brother, but he didn't know what to say to her. He felt awkward and unsure of himself and he didn't like feeling that way.

"Lisa, this is Cade Weston." Kate glanced from one to the other, bewilderment flickering in her blue eyes. There were strong undercurrents between Cade and Lisa. Kate was aware of the strain in Cade and wondered why he was so tense.

Lisa politely extended her hand toward Cade. "We've met before."

Cade paled again, remembering vividly when she had asked him to develop the oil prospects for Masters Corporation. His abruptness at that meeting might have driven a wedge between them that he didn't want.

Cade extended his hand to Lisa, then fit it into his pants pocket. There were so many things he wanted to say to his sister. Sister! He felt as though the wind had been knocked out of him. How many times when he was growing up had he wanted a brother or sister? Hundreds. Now that he had one he didn't know what to do about it.

"It's good to see you again, Lisa," Cade said awkwardly but meaning every word.

When he'd found out who his father was, he'd been jealous of Lisa. She had had what he hadn't—his father's name, his time and his love. But that feeling of jealousy had quickly died. He knew what kind of man Judd was, and from the rumors Cade had heard, Judd had tried to dominate Lisa's life, too. Their kinship went beyond being sister and brother.

Lisa's slate-gray eyes widened. She started to say something, then decided against it. Turning toward Kate, Lisa tried to smile again. "I just stopped by for a few minutes to say hello. I'd love to stay but I'm expected out at the ranch for dinner."

Cade stiffened, his hands clenching within his pockets.

"How's your father doing?" Kate asked.

"Getting better. Dad has finally decided life isn't all work, and he's actually resting." Lisa's hand tightened around the leather strap of her purse.

Lisa said all the right things, but Cade felt her growing distant. She was as skeptical of him as he was of her. They were two people afraid to test the water because they had been burned once before.

"I'm glad to hear that. Oh, Lisa, I see a friend about to leave. Wait just a minute before you go. I'll be right back."

For a moment Cade's gaze was on Kate, who was making her way through the crowd toward her friend. Then, afraid of what he would see in Lisa's eyes, he returned his regard to her.

"I didn't know you would be here," Lisa said, her tone slightly accusing.

"I deserved that." Cade paused, drawing an uncertain breath. "I'm sorry, Lisa."

"Cade, I . . ." She swallowed hard, her lashes concealing the indecision in her soft gray eyes. Abruptly she turned on her heel, whispering in a quavering voice, "Tell Kate I'll talk with her later."

Cade reached out to stop her from leaving, but his hand grasped only empty air. Ever since he talked with Ruth, he'd wanted to approach Lisa. He wasn't sure why, but he couldn't forget the picture his mother had painted of Lisa at the hospital waiting to see if Judd would be all right. There was deep sadness in his sister. Her life hadn't been any easier than his. She was as lonely as he.

Cade flexed his fingers as his hand dropped back to his side. Waiting for Kate to return, he stood apart. Empty. Alone. Like a tall sturdy oak on top of a hill, braving the elements, surviving against the odds. *Am I always going to be a loner? I have a sister I want to get to know. But how do I erase all those years that separated us?* Slowly and patiently, traits he wasn't well-known for having.

"Where did Lisa go in such a hurry?" Kate asked as she approached Cade, her brother beside her.

"She said she had to go and would talk with you another time," Cade answered absently, his gaze finally straying to the two people before him.

"I take it you're Cade Weston." Greg held out his hand.

"Yes." Cade focused his full attention on Greg and Kate, shaking the offered hand. There would come a time when he and Lisa would talk, Cade decided. She needed time to adjust to all that was happening to her. Running Masters Corporation while Judd was recovering and discovering she had a brother would be difficult for her to digest all at once.

"Kate tells me you're a geologist. Who do you work for?"

"Myself," Cade answered proudly, noting that Greg had inherited his father's charisma. It would take him to high places in government. Cade sensed he was a man to be trusted, a rare quality in a politician.

After Cade and Greg exchanged some views on the oil industry, Kate's brother left to circulate.

"I can see why your brother has little time for himself. It must be tough to have to be on your toes all the time, smiling, having to say the right thing," Cade said.

"I can't see you hitting the campaign trail. That isn't your style."

Cade tipped his head to one side, amusement in his eyes. "What is my style?"

"Oops. I think I stuck my foot in my mouth. Can I talk a guy into giving me a lift home?"

"It's not going to work, Kate. I'm not budging from this spot until I get an answer from you."

"Okay." She braced one hand on her hip, her chin lifting defiantly. "Crowds are definitely not your thing. And the only person you feel you have to answer to is Cade Weston. You stand back from the rest of us, observing but apart."

The serious expression on Cade's face canceled out his teasing look. "I've had little choice in those matters most of my life, Kate. Come on, I'll give you a ride home."

His tone told her that the subject of him was not open for further discussion. She managed a smile, but the uneasiness stayed with her as they walked toward his pickup.

Two hours later they were comfortably settled in two lounge chairs on her terrace, watching fireworks light up the heavens. For two hours they had talked, but they hadn't really discussed anything important. Small talk, Kate thought with frustration. And since the fireworks began, even the small talk had stopped. Cade sat in his chair sipping his drink and staring at the darkened sky.

Kate ran her fingertip along the rim of her glass. He's withdrawn, she thought, not knowing how to reach the private man beside her, but very much wanting to.

Cade placed his empty glass on the table next to him. Kate's presence beside him magnified the loneliness of his life. Having listened to Kate talk about her brother and her parents, he envied her. Her family was so close, while he didn't really feel he belonged anywhere completely. He had a sister he couldn't openly acknowledge and found hard to talk to. His father wanted to control him, not love him. For a brief time he had had a family when Rachel had been alive. But now with Matthew it was more as though they were friends. His son was growing up so fast and before long would be gone.

"Would you like another drink, Cade?"

Cade looked at Kate, her features hidden in the dark shadows of the balcony. The last rocket exploded in the sky, a brilliant multicolored illumination that momentarily revealed Kate's face. The concern he saw there twisted his heart. He hadn't fooled her with his diversions from his personal life. Didn't she understand there wasn't anything interesting to discuss? There was nothing there. Or perhaps she did. Kate saw things that many people who had known him a long time didn't, and that frightened him.

He wanted to reach out and grab the companionship Kate was offering him, but something was holding him back. His sense of fair play? With Kate the give-and-take would have to be fifty-fifty.

"No, I think I'd better be going. I've taken up enough of your time."

"What are you afraid of, Cade?"

He froze in the motion of standing and lowered himself back down onto the lounge chair, every action very controlled.

"We've sat here for two hours and you've avoided anything having to do with you personally. And frankly, Cade, I find the subject very interesting."

Cade inhaled a sharp breath. "You are blunt."

"I told you once I don't play games."

"I can't talk easily about myself." He moved to the railing with an ease that belied his troubled state. He said nothing, the only sounds the chorus of insects and the occasional passing car.

"It's me you're afraid of."

"When I'm around you I want to open up, but something holds me back." He shrugged. "I guess old habits die hard."

Kate stood beside him at the railing. "I suppose tonight is a time for reflection for both of us."

The sadness in her voice drew Cade to her. "Your husband?"

She nodded. "We used to spend the Fourth hiking in the mountains near a cabin my family owns. I always felt on top of the world going to that cabin."

His eyes were tender as he laid his hand over hers. "I may not talk much, but I'm a good listener, Kate. I've been where you are."

"Thomas is a part of my past, a past I'll always cherish, but life does move on. I've finally accepted that." She cupped his face in her free hand and smiled up into his eyes. "Thank you for caring, Cade. That means a lot to me."

"I envy your ability to speak your mind, to not be afraid to open up. Maybe you'll rub off on me." He brought her hand to his mouth and kissed each fingertip, his eyes still bound to hers. He paused at her forefinger and nibbled.

Kate thought she would melt when he crushed her against his chest, holding her tightly to him for a moment before closing his mouth over hers. There was nothing gentle about the kiss. It was full of hunger and suppressed desire, as though he were trying to imprint himself in her heart.

When he pulled away, setting her from him, his breathing was ragged as he caressed her arms. Then in slow motion he gathered her gently to him, pressing her head into his shoulder. His hands roamed restlessly over her back as he laid kisses in her hair.

This time when he parted from her, he walked toward the sliding glass door. Stopping, he turned, his body silhouetted by the light from the living room, his expression hidden from her. But she felt his raking appraisal in every fiber of her being. His look delved deep into her heart and stole it.

"I should thank *you* for caring."

Then he was gone. The sound of the front door closing drifted to her on the terrace. His last words paralyzed her. There had been such longing in his voice that her heart ached for him.

Chapter Four

Cade watched Howard Keyes walk through the dining room toward the table. If Howard invested in his prospect, it would be personal. His former employer had made it clear it would have nothing to do with Keyes Petroleum.

When the older man sat at the table, Cade said, "Let's order a drink. Then I'll show you my prospect, Howard."

After the waitress had left with their order, Cade opened his briefcase and removed the package that consisted of maps, cross sections and the economics of the deal. He spread the maps on the table and began to explain.

"As you can see from the maps of the few dry wells in the area, the data from their core samples indicate oil in the pores of the chips of rock brought up," Cade said, taking his glass from the waitress when she returned with their drinks.

Howard took several sips of his martini while he studied the maps and cross sections, asking a question from time to time.

"My lease is six hundred and forty acres. The pay sand runs about two hundred and fifty to three hundred acres in this area here." Cade pointed to a section on one of the maps. "I have all the land surrounding the area."

"What do you think you're likely to find in the pay sand?" Howard asked, finishing his drink.

"I figure two hundred thousand barrels of oil per forty-acre spacing. At fifteen dollars a barrel, that would be three million dollars for the life of the well."

"How many wells do you think will be in the prospect?" Howard signaled the waitress for another round.

"Six."

Howard's brow was furrowed in deep thought as he reexamined the maps and the economics. "Each well will cost approximately three hundred thousand, and you're looking for two investors to put up a third of the money each for twenty-five percent of the well."

"I'll put up the last third and have fifty percent."

A smile broke through Howard's thoughtful expression. "That sounds fair, Cade. Count me in for a third. We'll sign the papers next week and I'll arrange for the money to be put into your business account at the Denver Exchange Bank."

The waitress appeared with their second round of drinks, and Cade raised his glass in a toast, saying, "To a successful partnership."

After Howard toasted the new partnership, he finished his martini and rose. "I'm sorry I can't stay to celebrate, but you know how it goes. A group of investors came into town unexpectedly today, so I won't be able to stay for dinner. I have my own persuading to do."

"We'll get together when the first well comes in. I'll be in touch with you soon." Cade shook Howard's hand in farewell.

Cade was putting his maps back in his briefcase when a soft, feminine voice said behind him, "Isn't this a small world, Cade Weston?"

Kate was sitting in the chair next to him before he had closed his briefcase, smiling mischievously. Needing the time to collect himself, Cade slowly placed his briefcase on the floor. He still had a long way to go, but Howard had brought him one step closer.

But when he looked back at Kate, a smile radiated from him. *What the hell, Weston. You've had little to celebrate lately, so enjoy the moment while it lasts. Tomorrow you can start looking for the other investor.*

Kate's smile equaled his in brilliance. "I'm sorry I'm late. An emergency came up at the office. One always does when you're ready to leave. Has Howard gone already?"

"He had to woo his own investors."

"I don't need to ask if he's going to invest. I can see it on your face."

"And I thought I was the perfect man of mystery."

"About ninety-nine percent of the time."

"I'm going to have to work harder to control that one percent."

Suddenly Kate was no longer smiling. "I was hoping it was a sign. It's hard to understand a book when the pages are blank."

Cade stared at her for a moment, then threw back his head and laughed. "A book! I've been called many things in my life but never a book." When she continued not to smile, he reached across the small space that separated them and took her hand, his own expression sobering. "Kate, I don't trust easily. There are times I wish I was different, but I'm not. Things happen to a person that can destroy that."

"Tell me about your childhood."

Pulling his hand away from hers, Cade felt disconcerted. "My past is *history*, Kate."

His emphasis on the word "history" clearly shut her out. Kate started to speak but noticed the waitress hovering nearby, waiting to take their orders for dinner.

Cade followed her gaze and said tersely, "Let's order."

After they placed their orders with the waitress, silence fell between them. Kate took a sip of her water, then another. Cade nodded to someone he knew across the room. The chatter of the diners nearby and the clang of silverware and dishes contrasted sharply with their continual silence.

Kate put her glass down forcefully, the water splashing onto the tablecloth. "Every time we've been together you have masterfully avoided any subject that has to do with you personally. You know my whole life story and I know nothing past the facts on your loan application." This time it was Kate who reached across the table and took Cade's hand. "Was it that bad, Cade, that you can't talk about it?"

He tried to shrug off the feelings that were swamping him. Her small slender fingers, wrapped around his, riveted his thoughts to the desirable woman next to him. But not even her tactile presence could halt the other feelings that assailed him. Bad? There had been times it had been hell: an emotional hell to be rejected by your father, to have to prove yourself continually to others because you were a bastard and not quite good enough for them.

Cade stared down at their clasped hands, closing his eyes against the sight. "At times," he whispered finally, opening them and gazing again at their hands. There was a glimmer of torment on his face before a shutter fell into place, bringing back that blank look.

Mindful that they were sitting in a restaurant frequented by Cade's associates, Kate sandwiched his large, rough hand between her two smaller ones and wished they were somewhere private.

"Cade, I won't push you, but I want to know you, the man. Your past is how you arrived at who you are today."

His square jaw was set in a grim line.

"You can't keep running away from it, Cade. If you don't face it and come to terms with whatever it may be, someday it could destroy you, make you into a person you don't really want to be."

Cade looked beyond her. "What delayed you this evening?" he asked her as the waitress brought their dinners. The severity of his hawk-rugged features dimmed; a slow sensual grin crept onto his face.

Her mouth quirked at the corners. "Okay, Cade Weston, you've made your point. You win this round, but I have to warn you that I don't give up. The Stanfields are renowned for fighting to the end."

The corners of his eyes crinkled with deep laugh lines. "Kate, are you avoiding my question?"

Kate brushed back a wisp of hair that had fallen from the bun on top of her head. "I'm having trouble with a colleague at the bank. We don't see eye to eye on an important project." She wished she could tell Cade the rest, but the expansion plans weren't public knowledge. Samuel had drawn the battle lines in the executive meeting and had squared off to fight her every inch of the way.

Cade sensed the subject was closed and had to respect her privacy. They each had things they couldn't speak of, but with Kate he felt her reasons were professional, having nothing to do with her personal life.

"I have a golf date with Robert in a few days to discuss the oil prospect. We've already had one meeting. If he invests, I'll be able to start drilling right away."

As they ate their dinner, Cade discussed his meetings with Howard and Robert. Kate was aware that when it came to his business, Cade was an open book. But there was no crossing over into his personal life.

As they were sipping coffee after dinner, Kate said, "If Robert doesn't invest, my father is still interested."

"I'll keep that in mind," Cade answered stiffly, tension gripping him. "Ready to go?"

The relaxed atmosphere was gone like a magician's disappearing act. Silence prevailed between them as they left the restaurant.

In the elevator Cade leaned casually against the wall, arms folded across his chest. *Fool!* he told himself. If Robert doesn't invest, what's stopping you from going to Walter Stanfield for the money? Cade shoved himself away from the wall, all casual pretense fading. Damn, what a mess. I won't ask because I'm interested in Kate. *No way will I have Walter as my investor if I'm dating her.*

Fool! You're risking a dream on a dead-end relationship. You don't have anything to offer Kate but debts.

As Kate walked ahead of him off the elevator, Cade studied the gentle sway of her hips, her grace and elegance as she carried herself across the lobby. He wanted her as he had never wanted another woman. But the risks of becoming involved with Kate would be greater than drilling in an area where there were no other wells.

Walk away and don't look back, the warning flashed in his mind as he followed her to the doors. But he wasn't superhuman. It was very hard to ignore the desire she was arousing in him.

"Where did you park your car?" Cade asked as they stepped outside.

"It's at my house. My secretary picked me up this morning."

Cade eyed her suspiciously.

Kate laughed. "I have ulterior motives. I thought I would lure you to my house on the pretext of looking at my paintings, then ravish your body."

"In that case let's be on our way." A roguish look lurked behind his innocent expression.

Twenty minutes later Cade was trying to unlock her front door and having trouble with one of her dead-bolts.

"I don't think you have to worry about a break-in, not when you have trouble getting into your own house."

"Greg insisted I get another lock for my door, and I've had trouble with it since I got it. I should be grateful to have such a caring brother, but it can be a pain at times."

Cade didn't miss the love that sounded in Kate's voice. He wished he had that kind of relationship with Lisa, but so much had happened—or rather, not happened—between them that he doubted it was possible.

"Pull the door toward you as you turn the knob. That should work," Kate said, touching his arm.

The feel of her fingers on his arm burned through the fabric of his jacket. The heat of the summer day still lingered in the air, but the heat Cade felt bolt through his body had nothing to do with the temperature. He almost flinched away from her, he was so disturbed by her presence. It took all his willpower to stay and finish unlocking her door.

When Kate stepped in ahead of him, he wanted to leave before it was too late, and he wanted to stay because he had denied his growing attraction for this woman for too long.

This is crazy, insane. There's no place a relationship with her will go. But Cade found himself closing the door behind him and advancing farther into her living room.

The look in his eyes held Kate transfixed in the middle of the room, her purse slipping to the floor as his long strides brought him closer to her. The naked vulnerability in him tore at her, rending her emotions into pieces, much as she sensed his were at the moment. Sympathy blended with need, constricting her breathing.

"I should go, Kate." He stood very still, inches in front of her.

She wanted to touch him, but she was afraid he would flee into the night like a wild animal suddenly intruded upon.

"Don't, Cade. The day has been hell and I don't want to be alone right now."

"Do you want to talk?"

Part of her knew she should be angry that he was coaxing her to talk about her problems, while he steadfastly remained silent about his. But she did need to talk and she trusted him. She didn't know much about his life, but she knew a lot about his character. He would never betray her confidences.

"Yes. Do you want something to drink first? Coffee? Beer?"

A disarming smile curved his mouth. "A beer." She started to turn away when he caught her wrist. "And thanks for not throwing that question back in my face."

Cade went out onto the terrace, removed his jacket and tie and sat in a lounge chair. Darkness had fallen, lending an intimacy to the night. He wasn't sure if it was wise to stay out on the terrace with the velvet warmth of a July evening enticing his senses. Before he could go back inside, Kate was handing him his beer.

She reclined against the railing, her stance marked with weariness. "I suppose every job has its problems. Mine come in the form of one Samuel Coleman, who thinks I got where I am because of who I am, Kathleen Stanfield Dole, daughter of Senator Walter Stanfield, longtime friend of Robert Simon."

His hand clenched tightly, biting into the aluminum can. A sudden feeling of protectiveness assaulted him, but he swallowed the angry expletive and let her continue.

"No matter what I do he seems to find something to criticize. Samuel is good at his job and I'm good at mine, but I think that man would die before admitting that." Her voice rang with indignant rage at her co-worker. "Lately every big project at the bank has to be a fight between us. I'm getting tired of it."

When Cade saw her shoulders sag, he was on his feet and before her, his hands clamping around her upper arms. "One of the things I admire most about you, Kate, is your fighting spirit. Don't you dare give up. You can't. I've been there and you can't let down your guard or you'll hate yourself for giving in. You must go with what you believe in."

Her head came up at the vehemence that sounded in his voice. "Cade."

His name on her lips was a plea, and his heart missed a beat. *Damn you, Samuel Coleman, for doing this to Kate!*

With a tenderness he hadn't experienced in a long time, Cade held her tightly. His breathing became increasingly more difficult as seconds became minutes and her nearness did strange things to his emotions. His common sense was eroding away completely.

He closed his eyes and dragged shaky breaths into his lungs to cool the raging fever that was quickly consuming him. But the heat of the night only helped fuel his ardent desire for Kate. He tilted her chin up with his thumb, and his mouth came down to possess hers. With unbelievable gentleness his tongue forged its way into her mouth and investigated it thoroughly.

Kate felt at home within the shelter of his comforting arms. The firmness of his lips, the smooth hardness of his teeth and the warmth of his breath drugged her with the male essence of the man. Cade stirred her deeply and she wanted to capture the passion of his soul.

She tangled her fingers in his tawny hair and met his tongue with hers in an intimate duel. She was being drawn deeper and deeper into him, becoming lost in a bottomless well.

Parting slightly, their breaths still merging, Cade brought up his hands to frame her face, then plunged them into her hair, sending the pins flying. Her hair cascaded about her in waves of dark wildfire, the light from the living room catching the touches of red. Then one hand cupped the back of her neck while the other began to unbutton her blouse.

She closed her eyes to savor the exquisite moment, only for them to snap open when his hand pushed aside the flimsy lace of her bra and he bent to taste her. Kate moaned, swaying against the railing for support. Her legs were rapidly weakening.

When Cade lifted his head, the passionate tether of his smoldering gaze linked her to him as no ropes or chains could. Reverently, almost sadly, he grazed her cheek with his thumb, his gesture tender, his skin rough and callused. The thumb took a leisurely path downward to trace the outline of her still-tingling mouth, the graceful arch of her neck and the hollow of her throat, where he could feel the thundering beat of her pulse. His eyes and hand worshiped her.

She stopped his hand and fit it against her cheek. Turning, she kissed the palm, her tongue searing lazy sensuous circles.

"Cade, please stay," she whispered, her voice soft, sexy, tremulous.

Her words ripped through him. He had heard the slight uncertainty hidden within the request, and he grabbed at it, his last hope before he went under. She wanted him as much as he wanted her, but it hadn't been easy for her to ask him to stay because of their precarious future.

Cade's heart felt as though it would explode. He wanted her so badly, but it was a selfish feeling that he had to discard if he were to look at himself in the mirror the next morning.

He gently stroked her jawline before dropping his hands to his sides. "Kate—" his voice quavered and he swallowed hard before continuing "—I have nothing to offer you. It wouldn't be fair to you. You're very special and you deserve a man who can give you more than I can. If I stay, it would be a commitment I'm not ready for."

He picked up his jacket and tie from the lounge chair and was at the sliding glass door when he paused, his hand halting in midair, his eyes full of regret and sadness. *I could love her if I allowed myself to,* Cade thought. *Wrong time. Wrong guy.*

"I'm sorry, Kate," he murmured in a tender voice, embodied with a wincing pain.

Kate watched as he walked away in slow motion. She was motionless only for a few seconds before she heard the reverberating slam of her front door.

She had seen the war raging inside of him and she had lost. I hadn't thought it possible to fall in love again but I did, she thought. And he's telling me he's not capable of loving.

Chapter Five

It was an hour past dawn and the temperature was already seventy-five degrees and rising. A heat wave, Cade thought as he stepped up to the third hole and pressed his tee into the baked ground. The things he did to please a possible investor. Cade's mouth twisted with amusement. He didn't even like golf, but Robert Simon loved the sport and many successful deals were conducted on a golf course.

Cade placed his ball on the tee and positioned himself to swing at it. Shielding his eyes from the sun's glare, Cade followed the flight of his ball, noting where it landed.

"Not bad," Robert commented, getting ready for his shot. "If you played more often, you could be quite a golfer."

Cade waited until Robert's ball was sailing through the air before replying, "Football's more my game."

"Ah, yes, you played for Colorado about fourteen years ago. I've heard you set some impressive records."

They walked back to the cart and put their clubs in their bags. Driving toward his ball, Cade said, "I was never sure if Howard was more impressed with my football prowess or my knowledge as a geologist. I think I finally proved myself—as a geologist, that is."

"The oil prospect you've put together looks pretty good. I talked over the information you gave me with Howard and Judd Masters. I respect their opinions when it comes to oil."

Cade's eyes became sharp and piercing as he stared straight ahead. *Control yourself, Weston. Don't blow this deal because of Judd.*

For a moment Cade considered asking about Judd and the stipulation being removed from the loan. But if Judd wasn't responsible, then Robert might ask questions Cade wasn't ready to answer.

"They both agreed with me and when Howard said he was going to be your other investor, I decided to go in on the deal. We can sign the papers in a few days."

The hard look eased somewhat in Cade's eyes as he brought the cart to a stop by his ball. "The sooner we sign the papers, the quicker I can start drilling the first well."

"For this first well it's one hundred thousand each?"

Cade nodded, trying to contain his excitement at obtaining his last investor. But the first thought that came into his mind was calling Kate to celebrate over dinner. He could be drilling within the month!

"No problem. This will be a personal investment, of course, having nothing to do with the bank."

Elated, Cade withdrew an iron from his bag and quickly took his shot, then was back in the cart driving toward Robert's ball. When Cade stopped near the ball, the older man didn't get out of the cart. Cade twisted around to look at him, and alarm bolted through him. Robert was as white as his golf ball and clutching at his chest. He tried to speak but no words would come out.

"Take it easy, Robert. I'll get you back to the clubhouse." Cade drove the cart as fast as he could. Robert's face was pinched in a frown, his dark eyes clouded with pain.

At the clubhouse Cade, shouting for help, assisted Robert from the cart. Groaning, Robert placed his feet on the ground, then crumbled into Cade, his eyes fluttering closed. Cade laid him gently on the ground and felt for his pulse. There was none.

Everything happened so fast that all Cade could think of was each life-saving step he was doing to save Robert's life.

When the ambulance arrived fifteen minutes later, Cade gave up administering C.P.R. Robert Simon was dead. But the one thought that kept running through Cade's mind was: Judd had had a heart attack and he could have died like Robert.

Kate sat in the backseat of her parents' car as her father drove toward Robert's grave site. The shock of Robert's death had finally worn off and the chaos at the bank would have to be met and dealt with.

While the minister said a few last words, Kate's gaze shifted around the circle of mourners, resting only briefly on Samuel before moving on and stopping at Cade. As his gaze met hers, a guarded look entered his eyes.

He hadn't called in a week, since that night he'd walked out of her house. Crimson flushed her cheeks when she remembered how she had practically begged him to make love to her. Kate drew herself up, her chin lifting. She would not throw herself at him again. The next move was his. She looked away from the penetrating gaze that could read so much of her inner self.

But as Kate glanced away, the image of Cade, dressed in a navy-blue sports jacket and dark slacks, was branded in her memory. Would he make the next move? His expression had told her nothing, as usual.

Kate was so lost in her thoughts that her father had to touch her elbow firmly to indicate it was time to leave.

Kate wanted to say a few words to Martha before leaving, and she stepped toward the small group of people surrounding the Simon family.

"Hello, Kate," Cade said close to her ear.

Her heart began to beat a shade faster as she replied, "Hello, Cade. How have you been?"

So polite, like two strangers, Kate thought.

"Okay."

"I still can't believe Robert is dead. He had so many plans for the bank." Her eyes saddened as she thought about Robert's enthusiasm over the expansion. "I heard you and Robert were playing golf when he died."

Cade's face paled, his eyes fixed on a point beyond Kate. "One minute he was fine, the next he was gasping for breath. I felt so helpless."

She resisted the strong impulse to touch him. She had no right to. Veiling her desire to comfort Cade behind a screen of courtesy, she said, "Robert loved to play golf. Next to the bank, the golf course was his favorite place."

"He wanted to meet at the country club for our business conference so he could get a game in before going to work."

"Was he going to invest?"

Cade nodded, his expression unreadable.

Damn your untouchable attitude! Kate wanted to scream in frustration. Instead, she spoke in a calm, civil voice that betrayed none of her real feelings. "What are you going to do now?"

"Look for another investor," Cade stated flatly, respect for her cool attitude flashing in his eyes. "My hands are tied until I can come up with another hundred thousand."

Beneath the intensity of his gaze Kate understood Cade's hidden meaning. Their relationship would be placed on hold until his first well struck oil—if it did.

"Why don't you speak with my father before he has to return to Washington?"

"No!" Cade instantly answered.

"Why not, Cade? The Stanfields' money is as good as the Simons'."

Her quiet voice demanded an answer, but Cade only replied, "I have my reasons, Kate." He pivoted and walked toward his pickup truck.

Emotionally Cade had shut the door in her face again. Kate had known it wouldn't be easy to get her foot through that door, but she was wondering now if it was next to impossible. As she watched Cade move away, she tried to think of a way to break down that barrier.

Cade paused in front of Lisa and they exchanged a few words before Judd Masters approached the pair. Even twenty feet away Kate could see Cade's eyes changing to that sharp impaling black that spoke of his deep anger. He blatantly ignored Judd, something few men would dare. Instead, Cade said goodbye to Lisa, then abruptly turned, his strides rigid as he covered the last few feet to his truck.

Suddenly Kate remembered the meeting between Cade and Lisa at her parents' open house. Kate had the feeling that Cade knew Lisa—as well as Judd. Maybe Lisa could give her the answers to the hundreds of questions she had about Cade. Kate decided to call her friend and arrange a lunch date soon. She had never been so frustrated in her life. Her father had always told her that if she wanted something badly enough and worked hard enough at getting it, nothing was impossible. She was beginning to think Cade contradicted her father's theory.

Kate forced her thoughts away from Cade as she greeted Martha and the Simons' son, Clayton.

"If there's anything I can do, Mrs. Simon, please let me know," Kate said, then stepped aside to allow her mother and father to speak with Martha while she talked to Clayton.

"I'll be at the bank on Monday to assess the situation," Clayton said. "I need to meet with both you and Samuel. For now everything will be placed on hold. I talked with Samuel yesterday and he filled me in on what Dad was doing."

As Kate moved away from the Simons, she noticed Samuel Coleman pausing to say a few words to Martha. Kate wondered what Samuel had told Clayton and felt chilled in the heat of the August day.

Kate was breathless by the time she reached the mall where she and Lisa were to meet. Thrown together at Harvard, the two women had begun a friendship that survived years of separation while Lisa had lived in New York. When they first met they had done things together because they were both from Denver, but soon a deep bond of friendship had developed that had nothing to do with their hometown.

Their first meeting had been at a party for a mutual friend. Kate's first impression of Lisa had been of a cool reserve. Later Kate had learned it was really an innate shyness, a certain vulnerability. On the surface her friend had everything going for her—intelligence, beauty, a proud, graceful poise, wealth. But behind all that, Kate had discovered a very lonely woman. There had been a void, a need to be loved and accepted for herself, that to this day hadn't been filled.

"Sorry I'm late." Kate shrugged. "Traffic."

Lisa's eyes gleamed. "And I'm the one who's been away from Denver. That's why I started out fifteen minutes early."

Kate fell into step beside Lisa as they started toward the assorted fast-food joints surrounding the tables and chairs in the dining area.

"I had to go into the office this morning. Since Robert's death the atmosphere at the bank has been rapidly approaching the point of explosion."

Kate and Lisa decided to order deluxe baked potatoes covered with cheese, ham, sour cream, chives and butter. After paying for their lunches, they found a table and sat down.

"Who's going to explode?" Lisa asked before taking a bite of her potato.

"Me. And probably Samuel Coleman. We're the most likely candidates at the moment. But by the time the battle for the presidency is over, there could be other casualties."

Lisa's perceptive gaze assessed Kate. "It's really getting to you, isn't it?"

"Well, I've lost two pounds in ten days." But Kate wondered if she wasn't eating and sleeping because of the pressure at the bank or because she hadn't heard from Cade in over two weeks. It was a toss-up, but she finally decided Cade definitely had top billing.

"Is the bank the only reason?"

"I called you because I needed some answers and I'm doing all the answering," Kate said with a short laugh. "I never could keep anything from you. The bank is part of the reason. There are two executive vice-presidents, myself and Samuel. One of us will more than likely become president soon. The big question, of course, is who?"

"Do you want the presidency?"

Kate angled her head to one side and looked intently at her friend. "Who wouldn't? I went to college and graduate school and worked hard to prove myself and make it to the top. After Thomas's death, it was what kept me going. I love my work." But as she spoke, it was as if one part of her had stepped back and watched herself recite a rehearsed speech. She wondered whom she was trying to convince.

"You're good at your job—there's no doubt about that. But you want more than your work."

"I want Cade Weston," Kate stated with all the candor she was known for.

Lisa's eyes grew round, then blinked. She started to speak, swallowed visibly, then just stared at Kate with a stunned expression on her face.

"Lisa, what do you know about Cade?"

"I don't know..."

Kate held up her hand to silence Lisa. "Don't try to tell me you don't know him. There's something between you two."

"We've never dated," Lisa quickly said, her voice tight.

"No, that's not it." Kate shook her head, slowly, thoughtfully. "I've seen you two together several times and it's definitely not that. But you have a connection with Cade somehow, Lisa. I need to understand him." The last was spoken in a slightly desperate voice.

"I can't help you, Kate. I don't know him!"

Kate was puzzled by the sadly vehement tone in Lisa's voice. "But at the open house, the tension between you two was so thick you could have cut it with a knife."

Sighing deeply, Lisa explained, "That's because I tried to get him to work on some oil prospects for us several months ago. He refused."

"You're telling me Cade wouldn't! Why not?"

Lisa's gaze dropped to her plate as she toyed with her food. "Because he doesn't want to have anything to do with Judd."

"Why?"

"You're asking me questions I can't answer," Lisa snapped, exasperated. "You'll have to ask Cade. An explanation of his relationship with my father will have to come from him, not me."

Lisa concentrated all her attention on finishing her huge baked potato while Kate couldn't eat even a third of hers. Her stomach was knotted with frustration. Now she was even more perplexed. But there was nothing she could do until Cade chose to include her in his life. She felt totally helpless, unable to do anything but wait.

After finishing lunch they decided to shop and began to stroll through the mall, pausing every once in a while to browse through a store. Lisa avoided anything that had to do with Cade. When they stopped in front of a shop window that had bronze oil derricks on display, Lisa quickly moved on.

But Kate couldn't resist the temptation when they approached Ruth Weston's store, The Finer Things. Kate wanted to go inside. The store had a good reputation, selling work by local artists as well as accessories for the house. But the real reason Kate wanted to go inside was to see what Cade's mother looked like.

"Let's go in," Kate coaxed as Lisa started to walk past the store.

For a second Kate wondered about the trapped look that entered Lisa's eyes. The impression was so fleeting that Kate wasn't sure if she had read her friend correctly.

"It's a new store at the mall and I want to see what it has to offer." There was a hint of a plea in Kate's voice. "If you want, I could meet you in fifteen minutes in front of the bookstore."

Lisa looked at the entrance to The Finer Things. "No. I don't mind going inside. I've been curious, too."

Kate wondered if Lisa had been curious about the shop or about something else. She had said it almost absently, as if she were thinking about something entirely different than what they were talking about.

The petite woman who approached them had to be Ruth Weston. The woman's dark eyes were Cade's. When Ruth asked if they needed help, her voice was quiet and soft. She directed the question at Kate, so when Ruth's attention shifted to Lisa, surprise flickered in the older woman's eyes.

"It's nice to see you again, Lisa," Ruth said, a warm smile on her face.

"Thank you." Lisa glanced around and added politely, "This is a lovely shop."

"You haven't been here very long, have you?" Kate asked, looking from the older woman to her friend, aware of the underlying tension between them. Lisa had her hostess smile on and Ruth's eyes were penitent.

"No. Only six months." Ruth's look softened as she scanned her shop. "I used to be at a small shopping center a few miles from here."

Kate felt uncomfortable and regretted coming into the store. She felt as if she had opened Pandora's box but didn't know what she'd released. Ruth answered any questions they had, trying to ease the strained atmosphere, but Lisa never quite relaxed. Lisa was gracious, showing a genuine interest in several paintings by a local Indian artist, but Kate quickly realized that they had better move on.

Ruth watched the two women leave. She hadn't been prepared to see Judd's daughter again. Lisa wasn't petite like Anne, but she had her mother's coloring. Seeing her brought back memories of the first time Anne had visited her, when Cade was just a few months old.

Ruth closed her eyes and drifted back into the past. Life had been simpler, more carefree, when she and Judd had been dating. She had known of Judd's intense desire to be rich. She had shared his dreams with him and had hoped that one day she would be a part of them.

Before they became lovers, she and Judd had been good friends, growing up in the same neighborhood. As children and later as teenagers they had always been there for each other. She hadn't been able to sever that connection totally. Even now she had a special place in her heart for Judd. Finally, though, he was where he belonged—in her memories.

Strangely she understood why Judd had married Anne, and because she did understand, she could forgive him. But she couldn't forgive herself for mishandling the situation between father and son. For years she hadn't been able to let go of her dream. In not doing so she had greatly hurt Cade.

But dreams did not always come true, Ruth thought as she headed for her office in the back of the store. She couldn't change the past, but she could certainly try to change the future. She had been wrong in not letting Judd see Cade. It was time that father and son came to an understanding. She hoped it wasn't too late. Judd and Cade were both very stubborn. *But so am I,* Ruth thought with a bittersweet smile.

Cade and Judd had been estranged for too long, and Judd's heart attack had made her realize all that her son had missed by not knowing his father. She knew of the pain that Cade had silently endured, and she had tried to lessen it. Cade had even stayed in Denver for her sake, though he would never admit it.

She had watched her son slowly become closed to the people around him as he grew up. It had been his way of dealing with something he'd had little control over—his birth. Cade was afraid to trust anyone with his feelings and she couldn't blame anyone but herself. He was suffering for her mistakes.

Financially Cade would risk everything on an oil venture, but emotionally he was afraid to risk anything. In the business world he knew that to gain anything he had to gamble at times, but that had never transferred over into his personal life, except where Matthew was concerned.

Sitting down at her desk, Ruth picked up the phone to call Judd Masters for the first time since she'd told him she was expecting his child.

Chapter Six

"Does Cade know I'm going to be here?" Judd asked when he arrived at Ruth's house.

"No. He wouldn't have come if I had told him."

Judd raised a thick dark brow. "He didn't question you?"

"No. He's been very preoccupied lately with starting his company."

"I don't understand Cade. I told him I would loan him the money he needed."

Ruth smiled. "In many ways you two are alike."

Judd laughed bitterly. "I suppose so. Which means I should know him well enough to manage him." He sat down on the couch, none of the stress leaving his face.

Shaking her head slowly, Ruth asked, "Don't you know that's the worst thing you can do?"

Judd studied the plush brown carpet for a long moment, then looked up at Ruth. "I want my son's respect, Ruth." Suddenly Judd rose and walked to the picture window, his strides long and purposeful.

The heavy silence clawed away at Ruth's precarious composure.

His fist struck the wall next to the window, the sound reverberating throughout the room. "No, damn it, that's not what I want. I want my son's love."

His voice was low, barely audible, and Ruth knew how difficult it was for Judd to say that. He stared out the window, his back stiff, his arms rigid at his sides, as though he were battling with himself. She hadn't seen that stance since the day she had asked Judd to leave her and Cade alone because his marriage to Anne deserved a chance to succeed, and because each time Ruth saw Judd her life was torn apart. She had realized that if she didn't stop living in the past she would never be free of it.

"Somewhere along the line Cade has to accept me for what I am." Annoyance flared in Judd's eyes. "I won't apologize for what I am or for what I've done."

"You forget, Judd, I know you too well. I wouldn't ask you to."

For a long moment he looked her directly in the eyes; his expression softened. "No, I haven't forgotten anything, Ruth. While I was in the hospital I had a lot of time to think, I haven't always been proud of how I've managed the situation with you and Anne."

"We've both made our share of mistakes and have to handle our guilt the best way we can."

Judd rubbed the back of his neck. "I haven't done a very good job handling much of anything personal. While I was sick I took a good hard look at what I had. I have all the success a man could want, more than I dreamed of when we were growing up." A sardonic smile slashed across his features. "I had it all and my life was so damn empty. Lying in that hospital bed, I was finally truthful with myself. Power and money were all I thought I needed to make me happy."

"Things were rough when we grew up, Judd. I've known what has driven you all these years." Ruth absently smoothed the skirt of her dress over her legs. "Our past is what has driven me to work toward owning my own store and making it a success. No one likes being poor."

"But I sacrificed everything to have that money and power. I made a conscious decision not to give in to my emotions." Restless, Judd began to prowl about the room. "I was selfish. Still am, for that matter. I wanted both you and Anne, and once I thought I could have both of you. That selfish act nearly cost me my marriage and has cost me my son's love." Pausing, he turned toward Ruth. "I thought Anne didn't know about Cade. Things could have been different if I'd known Anne was aware of Cade's existence and understood. Or, I should say, loved me enough to forgive me."

"Judd, I couldn't take you coming from your wife to visit Cade."

Until she had sat with Anne waiting to see if Judd would live, Ruth realized she hadn't been totally free of him all those years. A small part of her had still grasped at what they could have had if only things had been different.

Through the long hours sitting in the waiting room at the hospital she had finally acknowledged that she had never allowed herself to come to terms with their situation. Instead she'd chosen to ignore and run from it. Thirty-four years ago she'd decided to avoid everything by denying Judd his fatherly rights. It had seemed the right thing to do at the time because she had done it to preserve her sanity.

"Why didn't you tell me that Anne came to see you after Cade was born?"

"It wasn't my place to tell you." She couldn't tell Judd of Anne's plea that Ruth give them a chance because Anne was expecting Judd's child. Ruth wasn't proud that she had clung to Judd, secretly hoping he would leave his wife to give his son his name.

Judd moved toward the window and braced an arm against the frame. "You know, I always saw love as a weakness. I always loved Anne, but until I was sick I would never admit it to her or myself. Then when she left me after my recovery, I knew that without her all the money and power meant nothing. I hurt her and I've hurt you, Ruth. But most of all I've hurt myself." Bending his head, he stared down at the windowsill. "I'm sorry, Ruth. I used the love I feel for you and our friendship as a barrier between myself and Anne. It was easier than facing the feelings I had for her."

Tears glimmered in Ruth's dark eyes. Judd had changed in the last few months. A year ago he would never have apologized, let alone admitted his mistakes. They both had changed from the teenagers who dreamed and talked of better times.

Slowly he faced her, his features pale, his expression pained. "You will always be special to me. That could never change. Our friendship goes back a long way. You've always been the stronger one. I hung on to your ghost and because I did, I never gave Anne a chance. Now that she's back, Anne and I have that chance. You and I are both free of our past, Ruth."

The front door opened and Judd and Ruth looked toward the hallway, each tensing for Cade's entrance.

"Mother, there's a car..." Cade's voice came to a halt when he saw Judd reclining against the windowsill, with his arms folded across his chest.

Cade started to leave when Ruth said, "Please stay, Cade. Don't you think it's time you sat down and talked to your father?"

"Why? What good would come of it? I've talked with him before." He blatantly ignored Judd standing only a few feet away. "Mother, you've never tried to meddle in my affairs before. Why are you starting now?" He felt Judd's eyes on him and he seethed with anger that the man would dare try to talk now after all these years.

"I know how you must feel, son, but..."

Cade rounded on Judd. "Do you? You have no right to call me son. I seriously doubt you have any idea how I feel. You don't know how to feel any kind of emotion, certainly not love. That word isn't even in your vocabulary. Look what you did to my mother. She doesn't date. She works all the time. I hoped somewhere along the line she'd become interested in another man and forget you once and for all."

Ruth's eyes widened. "Cade, between raising you and working to get enough money to buy my store I never had enough time. I haven't been dissatisfied with my life. The Finer Things is in an excellent location and doing very well. I have a son and grandson I adore. I have a wonderful set of friends and my work with the theater group. I lead a very busy life, Cade."

Judd pushed away impatiently from the windowsill. "Okay. I realize we can't be friends overnight, but why can't we start out by being business partners? I still need someone to develop those oil leases. I want you, Cade."

"But I don't want you. I know you contacted Robert Simon in regard to my loan. You can't buy me, Judd. Leave me alone."

Judd's eyes narrowed; his jawline hardened. "I don't want to buy you."

"Isn't that what you've been trying to do with the trust fund for college and this latest offer? And don't think I don't know about your recommendation to Howard Keyes when I graduated from Colorado. When I found out about that one I almost quit, but then I decided I had something to prove to everyone. Didn't you think I could get a good job on my own? After all, I graduated in the top ten of my class. Or did you think I was just some dumb football jock?'' Cade's voice was full of scorn.

"I knew what your grades were." Judd's growing anger was apparent in his dark glinting eyes.

"That's just it! You're constantly keeping tabs on me. I feel like my life isn't my own. You seem to know what's going on before I do. I don't want to be spied on. I don't want a damn thing from you!''

Cade felt the room closing in on him. He was shaking so badly inside that he knew he had to get out of there fast.

"I'll talk with you some other time, Mother, when it's less crowded in here." Cade pivoted and strode toward the front door.

When he stepped outside, hot air blasted him, adding fuel to the already heated emotions he was experiencing. With long angry strides, he headed for his truck. His hands were trembling, his body hot and cold. He clamped his fingers tightly around the plastic of the steering wheel, but nothing would stop the tremors.

Judd's face had been paler than usual, but otherwise he looked good. *Stop it!* Cade slammed a palm against the wheel, his inner rage making him indifferent to the pain.

Of course Judd looks good. He's a survivor, a user. People like him always come out on top. He used me when it benefited him to have a son. And he used my mother, discarding her like a worn-out shoe.

Before he found himself going back inside and completely losing his control, Cade started the engine and backed out of his mother's driveway. He drove with no conscious thought as to where he was going. When he pulled up in front of Kate's house, he braked and stared at its stone facade. He wasn't really surprised because he had known deep in his heart he would end up at Kate's.

He hadn't talked with her in over two weeks and he needed to now. He needed to be held. He needed this cold trembling to stop. He needed to feel close to another human being as he never had before.

But to love is to be hurt. Emotionally he didn't know if he could take any more hurt right now.

Kate sat at the desk in her living room and tried to write some checks to pay her bills, her thoughts wandering as they often had the past few weeks. Exasperated, she laid down her pen. Her life was definitely in an upheaval. First Cade and now her job.

She dreaded going into the bank tomorrow. First thing Monday morning Clayton Simon would meet with the executives of the bank to outline what would be happening over the next month. Of particular interest to her would be the procedure for finding a new president. Perhaps Clayton would want to fill that capacity now. The bank had always been his father's favorite enterprise. Maybe Clayton felt the same way.

Kate started to walk into the kitchen to refill her glass when the doorbell rang. She wasn't expecting anyone. Puzzled, she opened the door and nearly gasped.

Cade was leaning against the wall, his forearm braced against the door frame. The troubled darkness in his eyes threatened to consume her.

Kate glanced away from that probing gaze. The disarray of his hair caught her attention for a few seconds. It looked as if he had repeatedly run his fingers through it. But soon she was looking back into those anguished pools, and her heart throbbed. She ached to draw him into her arms, but she was afraid he would erect the No Trespassing sign again.

He straightened away from the wall, his eyes never leaving hers. "Hold me, Kate. Please hold me." His voice was a raw whisper that pierced through any resistance she had.

She held her arms open and he walked into them. He embraced her fiercely, as if he were hanging over a high cliff and she were his rope.

"Oh, God, Kate, you feel so good." There was naked agony in his husky voice as his arms wrapped even tighter about her. He buried his face in the silky mass of her hair and breathed in her unique scent.

They stayed locked in the embrace for a long time. Questions formed in Kate's mind but were quickly discarded as she felt Cade shudder from some terrible memory. He needed her and that was all that mattered. There would be time for questions—and answers—later.

Cade picked her up and, like a homing pigeon, headed straight for her bedroom. The burning intensity in his eyes ignited into a rampaging inferno as he settled her on the bed, then quickly shed his clothes. He knelt beside her and just as quickly undressed her.

Staring down at her, Cade realized he had to have something good in his life to hang on to. Kate was his life preserver, thrown to him during this stormy time. Fitting his long length beside hers, he pressed her to his hard chest and clung to her.

She felt the pounding of his heart against her breasts, felt his corded muscles tense like a coiled spring. She sensed his desperation.

He pulled slightly away, his heavily veiled look roaming over her features. Then he exploded. He tangled his fingers into her hair and planted feverish kisses all over her face, then ground his mouth into hers. The hard pressure of his mouth demanded and sought everything of her.

She should have been frightened by his intensity but she wasn't. It mirrored her own feelings, a hunger that had to be satisfied or it would leave her empty. She met his demands with her own, giving as he took, taking as he gave.

Her senses reeled at the feel of his tongue on hers, the rough texture of his hand on her skin, the heavy weight of his leg thrown over hers. He surrounded her with his distinctive scent, his perfect body. Each tender, rough touch was an exquisite caress that pushed her farther and farther toward a dizzying height of rapture.

Feelings were conveyed in heated responses. Needs were fulfilled. Wants no longer were denied. They came together in a wild frenzy of passion, savage and primitive.

It took Kate a long time to regain any semblance of rational control. She lay within the crook of his arm, her head resting on his rapidly rising chest, and listened to the frantic beating of his heart. Slowly their breathing returned to normal.

In a poignant gesture he raised her hand to his lips and kissed the palm softly, tenderly, in stark contrast to his ravenous lovemaking moments before. His lips moved in a tantalizing path to the pulse at her wrist and teased it with light flicks of his tongue.

This time they met in a gentle mating, slowly and tenderly drawing out each response within the other. He made love to her with his hands, mouth, eyes, the startling temperance of his caresses showing another level to his male sensuality.

The potent power of his lovemaking was heightened by sweet whispers of adoring praise. He told her everything he would like to do to her, his breath anointing her skin, the husky timbre of his voice erotic.

Her senses went wild; her heartbeat thundered in her ears. She was encapsulated in a mesh of spiraling sensations that sped her toward another realm that she never knew existed.

In turn Kate searched out all his hidden sensitive places, wanting to take him with her into that other world where colors exploded. She marveled at the hard, tough muscles that spoke of a man who loved the outdoors. She relished his tremor of response when she teased his male nipples, her tongue moist and gentle on his flesh.

When Cade positioned himself over her, his gaze fused with her passion-glazed one. Everything he couldn't express in words was in his eyes. Then slowly he lowered himself into her, sheathing himself deep within her.

Afterward, nestled against him, their bodies still dewed with perspiration, Kate toyed with the hair on his chest. "Cade, do you want to talk about it?"

For a long time he remained silent. Then he said, "I'm not ready, Kate."

The words were spoken so gently that Kate didn't feel that he was cutting himself off from her. He simply needed time to think things through, to sort out the confusion within him.

She propped herself up on one elbow and cupped his face with her free hand. "I'm here when you're ready."

His dark eyes were soft as a smile flirted with the corners of his mouth. He pressed her head against his chest and hugged her tightly to him.

"Will you go sailing with me next weekend?" Cade asked, his hand stroking her back.

"Yes," she murmured, knowing he had finally decided to give them a chance.

Chapter Seven

Lifting her face to the warming rays of the sun, Kate lounged on the towel spread out on the deck of the sailboat. The light breeze afforded some relief from the August heat. The gentle lapping of the water against the hull eased some of the stress produced by her hectic work schedule of the past week.

Through half-closed eyes she watched Cade guide the craft toward an isolated cove where they would drop anchor for the night. Her attention centered on his hand clasped around the tiller. Remembering those bewitching fingers traveling over her body, she felt a stirring in the pit of her stomach that feathered outward, heating her more than the sun ever could.

Cade is two different men, Kate decided as she succumbed to the lulling rock of the sailboat. There was the reserved, controlled man, who was a mystery she was solving little by little. But it wouldn't be easy to win his trust. He didn't give that often, perhaps never. Then there was the passionate, fiery man who gave so much of himself when they made love. He released the dam on his emotions for those special moments, and she hoped that through those actions, he was speaking of what was locked deep inside.

She slipped into a light sleep, with Cade monopolizing her dreamworld. Something warm and rough brushed her cheek. It had been such a long, exhausting week at work that she hated to awaken. But again a light glazing across her face urged her awake.

Her eyelids drifted halfway open, a dreamy, sensual look in her eyes. Cade was leaning over her with a crooked grin of mischief on his face. Her stomach flipped over at the playful gleam in his dark eyes.

Kate lifted her head and touched his chin tenderly before moving up to cup the nape of his neck. "I may trade in my alarm clock for you. It's much more pleasant than a loud buzzing sound."

His grin grew into a full-fledged smile. "I'll have to try it sometime. Do you know anyone who would like to apply for the job?"

"It depends," Kate said saucily, splaying her fingers across his chest.

"On what?" One brow rose inquiringly.

"Are you a pussycat or a lion in the morning?"

"Oh, definitely a lion until after the third cup of coffee. How about you?"

"A pussycat, of course. I like to purr and cuddle up to something warm. Do you have any suggestions on what that could be?"

"Possibly."

She felt the deep rumble of his laughter beneath her fingertips. The pleasing sound permeated the air with a delicious warmth. "I think I'll take my risk with the lion and apply," she murmured in a husky whisper.

"It would be the other way around, Kathleen Dole. I would be taking all the risk," he teased, kissing the tip of her nose, the corners of her mouth. "But then, I thrive on risk." His teeth caught her earlobe, creating delightful tingling sensations in her.

The first time Kate's stomach protested its hunger, Cade paused for only a brief second in nipping at the sensitive skin below her ear. But the second time it rumbled he pulled back and eyed her with a mockingly appalled look.

"Are you trying to tell me something?" he asked, amusement dancing in his eyes.

Shrugging, she sent him a helpless glance. "Well, I did forget to eat lunch today. I was working and lost track of time."

"But it's Saturday!"

"I know what day of the week it is." Straightening, Kate scooted back, wrapping her arms around her legs. "But there's a lot to be done. In case you haven't noticed, bankers' hours are no longer from nine to three Monday through Friday."

He reached out and caressed the skin under her eyes. "You aren't sleeping well at night. You're worried, Kate. I can see it in the shadows under your eyes. Is it over the battle for the presidency?"

The concern in his voice almost undid her. There were times like this that she was tired of being strong. Right now she wanted Cade to take care of her.

"Samuel Coleman isn't making this easy. He's determined to win at all costs. He's good at his job, I can give him that much. But he makes casual remarks that subtly undermine my authority."

"What will you do if he gets the job?"

Kate inhaled a deep breath and released it on a long sigh. "I don't know. I'll try to work with him, but in the past it's barely been tolerable."

Cade pushed to his feet and held his hand out to her. "Come on down into the galley and help me fix our dinner. By the time we prepare it, the sun should be setting and we can enjoy the view from up here."

"Why, Cade Weston, I do believe you're a romantic at heart. A quiet dinner on a sailboat in a peaceful cove watching the sunset. Is there wine, too?"

He grinned rakishly. "Champagne."

"I'm intrigued."

He pulled her up, one arm snaking around behind her to capture her against him. Through his shorts she felt his arousal and was thrilled at her effect on him. She wound her arms around his neck and looked up into his eyes sassily.

"Mmm. This is a side of you I haven't seen. It should be an extremely interesting evening." Kate lightly brushed her lips across his, then stepped out of his embrace to make her way toward the ladder that led below deck.

"If you don't watch it, you may see it sooner than you'd planned."

Cade watched the provocative sway of her hips as she walked. Her red shorts and navy-and-red halter were sexier than any bathing suit she could have worn. He liked the combination of confidence and sensuality in Kate. But he sensed that Coleman was definitely working at destroying her confidence. If he could get his hands on the man, he would teach Coleman a few lessons.

Kate stopped at the ladder and faced him with her hands on her hips. "I thought you were going to help, Cade Weston."

"Sorry, I was just contemplating wringing a guy's neck."

"I'm not sure I want to know who. I'd have a hard time telling a lie to the police. The truth is always written all over my face. My parents always knew when I was lying. Mother used to say there was a certain look in my eyes that gave me away."

Cade quickly covered the distance between them. "I'll have to keep that in mind."

As they descended to the galley, Kate asked, "Who?"

"I thought you didn't want to know." He chuckled softly.

"My curiosity is worse than a cat's."

"That bad," Cade said seriously, but the corners of his mouth quivered.

"Which got me into a few scrapes as I was growing up. Once, when I was ten, I rode my bike into an area that was off limits for me. My parents had set a boundary for me, but I just had to see who lived there, since the kids went to a different elementary school." Kate reached into the small refrigerator and withdrew the salad ingredients.

"Well, Greg saw me coming back from the 'forbidden zone and was going to tell if I didn't do his chores for a month. Greg became an absolute bear. After two days of being ordered around like a slave I told Mom. Her punishment had to be the lesser of two evils. Do you know Mom had known all along and had just been waiting for me to tell her myself?"

Cade paused in preparing the steaks for cooking. "You're very close to your brother."

Kate laughed. "How can you tell after that story?"

"I can hear the love in your voice." His throat felt tight. He had a sister but didn't know how to mend the fences. She had been denied him for so long that he'd given up hope.

"Having an older brother has its problems, but I wouldn't trade him for the world." Kate wrapped the cobs of corn in foil and handed them to Cade.

Cade was determined not to spoil the mood. Kate had problems; he had problems; but they would have to wait until Monday. "I'll put these steaks and corn on the grill, then open the champagne."

Kate watched Cade balance the tray and maneuver up the ladder. For a moment there she had lost him in some deep thought concerning family. She was determined to learn more about him this weekend. She had told Cade she was insatiably curious, and she was definitely curious about her man. She hadn't thought it was possible to fall in love again and she wasn't going to let him slip through her fingers.

By the time Cade came back down the ladder, she had made the spinach salad and the dressing. He stood behind her and slipped his arms around her.

He bit gently on her earlobe, whispering between nibbles, "You taste delicious. Are you sure you're hungry for food?"

She turned in his embrace. "Yes. I nearly ate everything for the salad before it got into the bowl."

"You can't blame a guy for trying," he said, his look that of a little boy who had been denied his candy.

"And I'm thirsty, too. Where's that champagne you promised me?"

Cade opened the bottle and grabbed two glasses to take out on deck. "The sun's going down."

Topside Kate sat down on the deck, leaning back against the railing, sipping her champagne and watching the colors change and fade. If she were writing a book, this would be the perfect setting for a romance. The sky was a vibrant splash of reds, oranges and purples. The soothing sound of the water and the quiet stillness of a summer's evening added to the serene moment.

Closing her eyes, Kate breathed deeply of the warm air. "I think I could stay here forever."

"I know what you mean. I miss having my own sailboat. This is peace."

"What happened to your boat?" She rolled her head to the side to look at his chiseled profile, his features gentle in the twilight.

He lifted his glass to his mouth and studied the darkening horizon. "I sold it last summer. Owning a sailboat took too much money. I have other priorities. Besides, Ted will lend me this one when he isn't using it."

"Your other priorities meaning your own company?"

He nodded, sipped his drink and continued to stare straight ahead.

She sensed him slipping away from her, but still she persisted. "Cade, what will you do if you don't make it?"

The lines in his face deepened. "I won't fail, Kate. I can't."

She set her glass down and touched his hand, feeling the tensed muscles beneath her fingertips.

"Cade, it's a possibility you have to accept. Only one in about fifty wells drilled is successful."

She felt a tremor pass through his body and was afraid she had pushed him too far. But he said nothing. Instead, Cade rose swiftly and moved to the grill to check on the steaks.

"They're ready. Let's eat." His voice was very controlled as he fixed their plates and returned to his seat.

The soft glow from the light below deck muted the strained lines on his face, but Kate felt his tension. She tried several times to start a conversation but after the third failure decided it was useless.

She was finishing her steak when suddenly Cade said, "Kate, I know there's a good possibility I will fail. I'd be a fool if I didn't know that." A rueful grin slanted across his mouth. "Some say I'm a fool for even trying. But I have to try until I have nothing left, or I'll always wonder if it was possible. What good will it do me to think I'm going to fail before I even drill my first ten feet?" He had a dream he had to pursue even if it meant losing it all, a need that drove him to succeed no matter what the costs were. How could he explain this to Kate when it was hard for him to understand it himself?

"I don't want to see you get hurt. And this means a lot to you." She would have given anything to mean as much to him.

"It's been a dream for a long time."

"What else has been a dream, Cade?"

Cade thought for a long moment. "Impossible things."

"But that's what dreams are made of."

Cade's expression hardened. "I only have one dream now. The others I gave up a long time ago when I discovered people could let you down."

"Dreams about your father?" Kate knew that his mother had never been married and realized the scars of being illegitimate could run deep.

"Yes."

His eyes narrowed to a piercing sharpness that denoted she had wandered into dangerous territory, but still she continued, "Do you know who your father is?"

"Yes," Cade snapped.

"Have you met him?" She must be insane. She could see his features turn to stone, but she had to ask. The anger inside him was an almost palpable force.

"Yes."

"Do you want to talk about him?"

"No!" he growled, his fingers digging into her upper arms. He hauled her against him, bringing his mouth down hard onto hers. "I don't want to talk at all," he added against her lips. The anger in him uncoiled like a snake as he ravished her mouth.

Kate twisted away from the grinding pressure. "No, Cade, not like this. You're too angry."

"You're damn right I am. Why in the hell do you keep asking me about my father? Aren't I good enough for you? After all, I am a bastard."

Kate yanked away from Cade and sat on her heels, defiantly facing him. "You are a bastard but not for the reason you think. I don't give a damn who your father is. But you do. It's been a stone around your neck all your life. When are you going to get rid of it?"

Cade shot to his feet. "It's none of your business."

"Oh, good, shut the door in my face," she taunted, beyond caring how far she pushed him. She stood, the small space between them electric with their rage.

"Okay, you want to know who my father is," Cade said in a quiet voice, the carved planes of his face aggressive, ruthless.

She clamped her hand over his mouth, her eyes wide. "No, Cade, not like this," she replied in a gentler voice, her anger vanishing. His eyes were black pinpoints as she stared up into them. Slowly she dropped her trembling hand away. "You have to want to tell me. I wish I hadn't forced the issue. I want you to trust me. It was my impatience speaking a moment ago. I can tell that it's a secret you haven't told many people. I think your relationship—or lack of one—with your father is the reason you're afraid to trust. I care, Cade. I care very much." *Perhaps too much for my own good,* she added silently. Her desperation had almost destroyed what little trust had developed between them.

She watched as a gamut of emotions came and went in his eyes and prayed she wouldn't see that unreadable expression in them. "Cade, I grew up the same time you did. I know how cruel children can be to other children. I don't condone judging an innocent person for something he had no control over. But it does eat at you."

When he framed her face with his large hands, all the anger in his features was gone. Relief enveloped her. A tender smile entered her senses like cognac, intoxicating, enchanting, calming.

Slowly his mouth took hers in a gentle persuasion, his arms entwining around her, melding her to him. The passionate, tender Cade held her now. The taut brackets at the corners of his mouth were smoothed away, and there was a smoky, sexy glint in his eyes that sought to erase the anger between them.

"Oh, Kate, I'm not sure what to do where you're concerned. There aren't many people who can arouse my anger—or my passion—like you can."

"Love me. Hold me and make mad, passionate love to me all night long."

He stared down at her, his forearms resting on her shoulders. "Well, hon, I can hold you. I can make mad, passionate love to you. But I'm not sure about the all-night-long part."

She laughed up at him, locking her arms around his chest. "Two out of three ain't bad."

The creases at the edges of his mouth were deep with laughter as he pulled her to him, his mouth settling over hers in a soft conquest. The interior of her mouth was searched thoroughly and erotically.

Biting gently on her lower lip, Cade murmured in a deliciously sexy growl, "Maybe I can make it three out of three, after all."

"We'll take things one step at a time." Kate meant it on more than one level. Cade would run scared if he felt pressured.

"Let's go below," he whispered into her ear as he kissed its shell.

"If you keep that up, I'll never make it below." Her legs felt like water.

"That's okay, I was a star football player, and we dudes are tough."

"Cade, that was fourteen years ago."

Suddenly he scooped her up into his arms and headed for the ladder. "Lady, that was a challenge I couldn't resist."

"Cade! Watch your step. You'd better put me down." Each sentence was spoken between bursts of laughter. Cade was having a difficult time maneuvering her down the narrow passageway.

"There's got to be a secret to this. It works in the movies."

"Cade..."

He lost his balance near the bottom, and they toppled to the carpeted deck. Their laughter bonded them in a moment meant to be cherished. Cade rolled over and pinned her to the carpet, his hands on either side of her head. Kate's laughter died in her throat as Cade looked deeply into her eyes with a mind-shattering intensity.

His mouth descended to claim hers. The kiss was rough and gentle, demanding and persuading. His tongue flicked along her teeth, parted them and plunged into her mouth, circling with tantalizing finesse.

Cade stood and tugged Kate to her feet, drawing her against him. Burying his face in the fragrant softness of her hair, he worked loose the knots that held her halter together. It fell to the deck, exposing her breasts to his ardent gaze.

The sharp intake of his breath was a testimony to his aroused state as he brought his hands up to cup her breasts. Leaning over, he took a nipple into his mouth and suckled. Kate threw back her head, eyes closed, and relished the sweet rapture that gripped her.

Cade's hand went to the snap of her shorts and unfastened it. Slowly he lowered the zipper, then pushed his hand inside to caress her stomach. Moving downward, he found her core of womanhood moist and ready.

"This is what I dream about at night. I lie awake thinking about the feel of you, the taste of you. God, woman, you torment me," Cade rasped, his voice a thread of longing.

"Cade, do you think I'm immune to you? I love you, darling."

The arms around her tensed. "Oh, Kate, I could hurt you badly."

She hugged him tightly to her. "I'm a big girl, Cade. I know the risks in this venture."

When he looked down at her, her heart constricted at the haze of despair in his eyes. "I don't think you do."

"Make love to me, Cade," she pleaded, her body quivering with her need.

"I couldn't stop now if I wanted to."

Kate helped him undress as he helped her. The one light in the cabin illuminated them in a pale-golden sheen as they lay on the bunk, their legs entwined, their bodies pressed together. In that glorious moment when they were one, Kate's heart and soul fused and became a part of Cade. Without him she would never truly be complete again.

In the aftermath of their lovemaking, before she drifted into a deep sleep, Kate dimly thought that she shouldn't have told Cade yet that she loved him. She prayed that the following morning she wouldn't find the door closed again on his inner self.

Kate reached out and touched the still-warm space next to her, blindly searching for Cade. Her eyes flew open. He was gone; the cabin was empty. Concern and panic surged through her, sending her flying from the bunk.

Slipping on her clothes, she kept thinking that she shouldn't have said that she loved him. She had wanted to wake up with him next to her, but instead, he had left her side sometime during the night.

Cade, clad only in a pair of shorts, stood on deck, leaning on the railing. The brilliant colors of a new day were marred by clouds rolling in. She moved to his side and laid her hand on his shoulder.

"Cade?" Her voice quavered with her uncertainty.

He covered her hand with his and turned to her. The expression on his face equaled hers in uncertainty. "I don't deserve you, Kate."

He slid his arm about her shoulders and cradled her to his side. Staring out over the water, he began to speak in a voice that was riddled with despair. "My father is Judd Masters."

Somehow the knowledge that Judd was Cade's father didn't surprise Kate. Over the past few months the elusive evidence had been there in the back of her mind, but she hadn't allowed herself to piece it together.

"When I was growing up, I used to dream that my father would return to marry my mother and make everything right. When she finally told me who my father was, it wasn't easy for her. I don't think she was aware of how much her voice shook or of the pain in her eyes. But I'll never forget it. Judd Masters hurt my mother and for eighteen years he completely ignored me until I became class valedictorian. I still can't believe he thought I would welcome him into my life because he had a very small part in my conception, then completely turned his back on what made a real father. Growing up I found it easier to think of my father as dead and to hold on to the dreams of what I thought a father should be. Dreams didn't hurt—or reject."

Cade shut his eyes and swallowed the tight ache in his throat. "Not many people know that I'm Judd's bastard." The bitterness in his voice spilled over into his expression when he opened his eyes.

Kate inhaled a deep breath, but still she felt as though she was suffocating. The tormented agony in his voice knifed into her. She understood a lot about Cade now. Judd Masters was a relentless, forceful man who overwhelmed the people around him. Cade was fighting for his own identity.

A gentle shower began to wash over them as they stood at the railing, separated from the rest of the world. When they both were shivering, they walked hand in hand to the ladder and descended below deck, the sound of the softly falling rain setting the pace for their lovemaking.

Chapter Eight

Sitting back on his haunches, Cade studied his son. Matthew was hammering the last board of the fort's floor into place. Whenever his son was deep in thought, his brow would wrinkle, his blue eyes would darken and his mouth would turn downward slightly at the corners.

Cade was proud of his son, but lately his fear of losing him was growing stronger. It was a feeling he used to be able to ignore. He loved Matthew so much. But it was that love that made him feel so afraid, so vulnerable. The very thought of losing Matthew felt like a knife ripping through him.

Cade wiped the sweat from his brow and rose. He walked to the cooler on the covered patio and withdrew a soft drink for Matthew and a beer for himself.

"Let's take a break, son." Cade handed Matthew his soda.

Matthew hopped down from the fort and stood back to survey their work, his chest thrust out proudly. "Dad, this is gonna be the neatest fort. Wait till my friends see it."

"I had a fort exactly like this one. Grandma had the hardest time getting me down for supper. In fact, I moved a lot of my things out to it."

Matthew cocked his head to one side. "Yeah, Grandma told me about having to bribe you to come in at night. I guess she hated being alone."

A sharp pain cut through Cade. At times when he was growing up he had seen his mother's eyes full of sorrow, and knowing she was lonely had made him always want to be there for her. But for a long time he hadn't known why—until she told him about his father. Then everything had fallen into place.

"No one likes being alone," Cade said finally.

"Is that why you're seeing Kate?"

Cade smiled and tousled his son's hair. "Can't put anything over on you."

"I like Kate, Dad."

"I like her, too," Cade murmured, hugging his son. *And that's the problem,* he added silently. *I like her way too much for my own good.*

"Well, I hope you two men are hungry. I think I bought the hamburger place out." Kate's arms were full of several sacks of food.

"It's about time you came back. We were about to faint from hunger. What took you so long? It's way past lunchtime." Cade forced himself to be cheerful.

"I think everyone in Denver is heading for the mountains. The traffic heading out of town was horrendous." Kate dropped the sacks on the redwood table, her attention drawn to the finished fort. "That looks great! I knew if I stayed away long enough I wouldn't have to do any work."

"Oh, but we saved a job just for you." Cade delved into the sacks and began handing out the food to Kate and Matthew.

Kate eyed him suspiciously. "What job?"

"You'll have to wait, Mrs. Dole." Cade ignored her pout and started eating his hamburger.

After lunch, Cade informed Kate she had the honor of painting the name of the fort on the sign. After much deliberation, they settled on the name Wild Wild West.

With a flourish, she dotted the two *I*'s and said, "There. What do you think? Should I go into the sign-making business?"

Cade and Matthew looked at each other and laughed. "No," they said between bouts of laughter.

Kate backed up a few steps to examine her work. "It is a bit lopsided, but other than that it looks fine." She tried to instill some confidence into her voice, but still she sounded doubtful.

"You can barely see the last word it's so squashed together." With a supreme effort Cade managed to stop laughing.

"I ran out of room. You should have made the fort bigger or come up with a shorter name."

"Or, Kate, my dear, you should have spaced your letters."

"Penmanship wasn't my best subject in school," she retorted, lifting her chin and spinning away from the amused pair to clean up the table.

While Matthew and Cade were picking up the tools and scraps of lumber, Kate took the trash into the kitchen. She stood at the sink and watched from the window as Cade and Matthew worked side by side in the backyard. There was a lot of love inside Cade and he showed that love to his son. She prayed one day Cade would openly show his love to her.

Turning away from the family scene, Kate left the kitchen, noticing her surroundings with an intense interest. That morning was the first time she'd been to Cade's house. They had always stayed at hers.

The house was sparsely furnished with heavy oak pieces. The earth tones were warm and inviting, however, and the few personal touches were definitely Cade. There was a picture of an oil derrick on the wall, and next to it on the mantel stood a large Colorado mug with a bronzed cowboy on a bucking horse.

"When do we have to be at Greg's political rally?" Cade asked from the sliding glass door. He stepped into the air-conditioned house, wiping his brow as he advanced toward her.

"In an hour. I have to help with the recruitment of volunteers for Greg's campaign. I was volunteered," she said with a laugh.

Cade slipped his arms around her and pulled her close. "Mother's picking up Matthew at the rally. I'm free tonight," he said with the eager anticipation of a child on Christmas morning.

"Do you have something in mind?"

His dark brown eyes sparkled. "Mmm. I thought I might go to bed early tonight. All this work today has worn me out."

"Oh, well, then, what I have in mind wouldn't work," she retorted in a flippant voice, her eyes gleaming devilishly.

He pinned her to him in a loose hold. "Just what did you have in mind, woman?"

She shrugged. "Isn't that academic now?"

"Lady, you're walking a thin tightrope. If you don't want to be the cause of my son's early sex education, you'll tell me." The mock menace roughened his voice to a low growl.

Sensing his deep arousal, she smiled up at him, the mischief in her eyes replaced by her own desire. "I have no intention of letting you leave my house tonight, Cade Weston," she answered in a seductive voice.

"Good, because I wasn't going to. All week the only thing I could think of was getting you alone in bed."

With the sudden reminder of Cade's absence all week, Kate became serious. "Did you have any success on your trip? We haven't had a chance to talk since you returned. I know it's something you don't want to discuss in front of Matthew."

He frowned. "No. I spent most of the week in Colorado Springs talking to some men about investing, and all they could tell me at the end was that the venture was too risky." One side of his mouth lifted. "They did wish me luck, though. And, Kate, I'm going to need it."

This was the first time she had heard even a hint of defeat in his voice. "I know the pressure can get to the best of us. Just hang in there. I have faith in you, Cade."

He grazed his knuckles over her cheek, the tenderness in his eyes silky and caressing. "How about you? Has Coleman been giving you trouble?"

"No more than usual."

"When will the board make a decision about the presidency?" His hand trailed around to the back of her neck.

"In a few weeks. I wish it were tomorrow. The waiting is killing me. Sometimes I'm afraid to make a decision. But Clayton Simon doesn't want to rush into something that's so important to the bank and his family. I understand, but it still isn't easy on my nerves." Kate tried to smile and dismiss it lightly but she couldn't. She felt like someone who was standing in front of a firing squad waiting for the trigger to be pulled.

Cade lowered his head and kissed her, imparting his quiet strength to her. "The waiting is always the worst part, even if the answer is bad. Once you know the answer you can handle it, but it's the uncertainty that puts you in turmoil. Your life isn't your own."

With their foreheads touching, they savored the shared moment of kinship. They were both playing the waiting game, a game that could affect the rest of their lives. Kate realized, though, that it was more than the job she was waiting for. The most important waiting game involved Cade, and as with the other, she had little control over the outcome.

The sound of the sliding glass door opening parted them, and Cade turned toward Matthew, who was entering the house. "Are you ready to go, son?"

Matthew nodded. "I packed when I got up this morning."

"We'd better get moving. I just need to change clothes and I suggest you do the same, Matthew."

Later, on the expressway, Cade automatically braced himself as he passed the newly constructed Masters building. He felt like a voodoo doll and every time he saw the Masters name on the sign another needle was being stuck into him.

Cade tried to concentrate on Kate and Matthew, who were discussing football versus soccer as a sport, but their words just flowed over him. With a great effort he steered his thoughts away from his anger and toward something entirely different, his oil prospect.

The past week had been fruitless. In the past month he had turned up only dead ends in his search for his second investor. He couldn't do a thing until he found one and he didn't know where else to look. He had exhausted his best contacts in the state. Money was tight.

Cade parked his truck in the lot next to the hotel where the rally was being held. As they walked into the building, Matthew stopped to gaze down at the people skating below them.

"Now, that's not a bad idea on a hot day like this. Maybe we should go ice-skating after the rally, Cade." Kate leaned over the railing to watch a father teach his young daughter how to skate.

Cade bent close to Kate's ear and whispered, "I've come up with a much better way to keep cool where I don't have to risk breaking my neck."

His warm breath tickled her neck, and she tried to think of a way to un-volunteer herself from the rally. She could think of a few ways of keeping cool herself.

"Dad, do you know how to ice-skate? A few kids at school are on an ice-hockey team."

"That's one sport I never could get my body interested in. My ankles refuse to support the rest of me."

"Maybe you just didn't have the right teacher." Kate laughed, though she tried not to. She could picture Cade skating with his ankles folding in on him. "I used to skate a lot in my younger days."

"I think I'll forgo that particular pleasure, but I'm sure I can come up with something else you can instruct me in." Playfulness shone deep in his dark eyes.

"I just bet you could."

"Come on. The quicker you do your duty, the quicker we can begin the lesson." Cade's voice lowered several octaves. His eyelids veiled his expression, but not before Kate had seen the temptation in his look.

They rode the escalator to the ground floor, where the rally was being held in one of the hotel's conference rooms.

"I can never resist doing this." Kate paused at the marble fountain near the escalator and threw a coin into the water, making a wish that one day she and Cade would be teaching their child how to skate or play football.

"What did you wish for?" Cade asked.

"Dad, she can't tell you or it won't come true."

"Right. You know better than to even ask, Cade Weston. I'm not saying a thing because I don't want anything to spoil this wish."

Inside the Colorado Room, Kate was immediately whisked away to help with recruitment. Kate sent Cade a look that said she didn't know when she would see him again.

He watched Kate talking with Greg across the room. Kate placed a hand on Greg's shoulder in a tender expression of sisterly love and Cade looked away. Kate was so open with her feelings. There were times he wished he could be.

"Dad, I see Grandma. I'll be back in a minute." Matthew hurried toward his grandmother.

Cade scanned the large room, nodding hello to a few acquaintances. His gaze came to an abrupt stop at the buffet table. Lisa was standing by herself. He hesitated for a moment, then headed straight for her.

"Hello, Lisa. How have you been?"

Cade shifted his weight from one foot to the other. He was the one who had started their relationship off on a bad note and he was the one to do something about it. Being around Kate made him realize that.

Lisa straightened, an air of distant coolness manifested in her stance. But deep in her smoky-gray eyes, Cade saw a flicker of uncertainty.

"I'm fine," Lisa answered, the aloof control she was noted for completely in place now.

"Are you supporting Greg for Congress?" Even to his own ears his voice sounded distantly polite, and he winced inwardly.

"No, I'm supporting Linda Peters." Lisa fingered the strand of pearls around her neck.

Cade's gaze was drawn to Lisa's hand, and he noticed that it wasn't steady. His attention flew back to her face, and in that second a silent message was communicated between sister and brother.

"Lisa—" He had so much to say, but it had been locked away in his heart for so long he didn't know how to say it. Unsure of himself, he asked instead, "If you're supporting Linda Peters, then why are you here?"

"Dad asked me to come."

"And do you always do what Judd wants?" He hadn't meant to sound so condemning.

"No!" Her gray eyes held storm clouds.

Sighing deeply with frustration, Cade tunneled his fingers through his hair. "I'm not very good at this, Lisa. Every time I open my mouth around you, I seem to stick my foot in it."

One corner of her mouth twitched; her slightly slanted eyes lightened to a silver gray. "Yes, you do."

"Could we possibly erase the last thirty-odd years and start fresh?"

She shook her head, the metallic silver in her eyes softening to a dove gray. "I don't think that's possible, but, Cade, they don't really mean anything. We're victims of a situation we have no control over. That shouldn't stand in the way of us getting to know each other."

Cade searched for a way to tell her how he felt. He looked beyond her at the table laden with food. "I always wanted a brother or sister." His gaze returned to Lisa's. "I still do."

There was a long pause before Lisa said, "I don't know much about you, Cade. May we get together sometime to talk?"

"I'd like that."

Lisa glanced behind Cade, saying, "Matthew's on his way over. It's hard for me to believe I have a nephew. He's a fine-looking boy, Cade."

"Matthew is a good son." His words were slow and full of pride.

Cade and Lisa didn't know each other well at all, but this was a beginning that he was content with. There was a lot that he wanted his sister to know but it would take time and trust, and he sensed she didn't trust easily, either.

"Does he know about us?"

"Not yet."

When Matthew and Ruth joined them, Cade introduced his son to Lisa, seeing the interest in her eyes as she shook Matthew's hand.

"We didn't mean to interrupt, but Matthew wanted to say goodbye," Ruth offered in explanation. "I have to go to the theater and work on some last-minute preparations."

"You didn't interrupt. Lisa and I were just talking about who we're supporting in the congressional race." Cade liked the sound of "Lisa and I." Maybe in time they would be as close as Kate and her brother.

After Matthew and Ruth left, Lisa went to speak with a friend. The crowd at the rally pressed in on Cade. Seeking the quiet of the lobby, Cade stood at a large picture window, staring at the asphalt street.

"Cade."

Cade pivoted, instantly wary.

Judd stepped forward, stopping a few feet away. His large muscular frame and the air of power and authority demanded attention.

Cade's emotions were frayed from the rough weeks of looking for an investor. "I don't have anything to say to you."

"But I do," Judd replied in a tone that was edged with impetuousness.

Not wanting anyone to overhear the conversation that Judd so obviously intended to have, Cade moved into a private alcove near the picture window and leaned against the glass wall. He tried to insulate his emotions in a case of ice, to school his features into blankness.

"I know Robert Simon was going to be your second investor and that Clayton doesn't feel he can invest the family's money in your oil venture at this time. You're looking hard to find a replacement for Robert, but you've nearly exhausted your resources."

A cold smile, full of mockery, curved Cade's mouth. "That crystal ball again?"

"I have my ways of finding out about someone I care about."

Cade laughed, the sound chilling. "You? Care? Never! Money and power have been all you've cared about. They've been your bedfellows all these years."

"Don't tell me what I feel and don't feel, Cade." Judd's voice lowered to a deadly level; his mouth compressed into a tight, thin line.

Judd was right. How could he tell Judd what he felt when Cade didn't know how he felt about anything himself? He was so mixed-up inside; the ice around his emotions was melting under his heated feelings toward Judd.

"You and I are a lot alike, Cade. I don't give up on something if it means a lot to me. I want to be your other investor."

Fire blazed in Cade's eyes. "All I ever wanted from you was to be left alone and to be able to lead my own life."

"Are you so sure that's completely true? You hate me for what you think I did to you and Ruth. But do you really, Cade? Do you really know all the facts, my side of the story?"

"Yes!" Cade straightened, his stance menacing, his hands jammed deeply into his pockets to conceal their trembling. "First you try to run my life and now you're trying to tell me how I feel about you. Next you'll be planning my marriage," he said sarcastically.

Judd paled; his jaw was a grim line. "No, actually I think you're doing a good job yourself. Kate Dole would be good for you and your career. I could never understand why you married that half-breed."

Cade's chest constricted, cutting off his breath. He burned with rage. "Leave Kate and Rachel out of this."

"I only want the best for my son."

Son! The word vibrated through Cade's mind. "Any stud can create a son, but that doesn't automatically make him a father."

Judd's eyes glazed. His hand made a hard, tight fist and his arm jerked. Cade tensed, preparing himself for the blow. Slowly, though, Judd's eyes took on an expression of controlled coldness and his hand relaxed.

"Kate has the breeding and money to help you tremendously," Judd said in a frigid voice.

Cade flinched from the meaning of Judd's words. "Breeding! Kate isn't a thoroughbred horse on your ranch. Not everyone has to marry a blooded filly to get ahead in this world."

Razor-sharp tension pulsated in the air as Judd glared at Cade. "I said we're alike. Kate's just as much a thoroughbred as Anne."

Cade recoiled, stepping away. He felt as though Judd had punched him in the gut. He pushed past Judd, his only thought escape.

Chapter Nine

Cade was halfway to the escalator when he came to a sudden halt. He'd forgotten about Kate. Reluctantly he made his way back to the Colorado Room.

Pausing inside the door, Cade scanned the room for Kate, his hands in his pockets. He didn't dare take them out. They were shaking too hard.

His gaze briefly rested on Lisa and fleetingly he thought of speaking with her. But his common sense pushed that idea out of his mind. The sooner he left, the better he would be. Right now all he wanted was to see Kate. God, he needed her desperately!

He located Kate sitting at a table signing up volunteers for various jobs in Greg's campaign. He placed his hand on Kate's shoulder and squeezed, compelling her to look up at him.

"And what job would you like, sir?"

Kate's smile melted some of the ice, but his heart still pounded with anger and a hot tightness clawed at his throat.

"I'm fresh out of empire-building jobs, but..." Kate's voice faded at the bare, wounded look in Cade's eyes.

He leaned down and whispered, "Can we leave now?"

The silent plea in Cade's voice prompted her to nod. Turning to the volunteer next to her, Kate said, "I have to leave. Can you handle this table alone?"

"No problem, Kate. Is something wrong?"

"No." Kate's smile was too bright. "The speeches are about to start and I never could sit through them. Greg may have to trade in his kid sister for a new one."

Kate gathered up her purse, thinking that something was terribly wrong. The anxiety sliced deep into Cade. She wanted to wipe the tormented look from his eyes. Her heart wrenched at the anguish she had briefly glimpsed before he hid it behind a mask.

Cade towered over her, taking in every feature of her face as if she were a map he was carefully examining.

She was confused and frightened, not of Cade but of the hurt he was suffering. She loved him but he was so determined to fight his battles alone. Would he ever realize it was easier to share the burdens?

Kate rose. "Where do you want to go?" She wanted to tease him and make him forget his worries, but whatever was eating at him went very deep.

"Anywhere but here." The impatience in his voice didn't completely cover the other feelings that were warring for supremacy.

"Let's go to my place."

He took her elbow in a firm grip as they walked toward the doors. He was reaching for the handle when Lisa spoke behind them.

"Cade?" There were many unanswered questions in that one word.

Cade slowly faced Lisa, the bleakness that had been hinted at earlier strongly etched into his features now. "We'll talk another time, Lisa."

Until that moment Kate hadn't really thought beyond the fact that Judd Masters was Cade's father. Now, though, the realization that Lisa was Cade's sister jolted through her. Looking at the two, Kate saw similar qualities in them that were also Judd's: the look of authority in their eyes; the way they held themselves, proud, distant, apart; the air of shrewd keenness that conveyed their intelligence; their mouths when set in an unyielding line.

"Call me, Cade," Lisa said, her voice quavering slightly.

His grip on Kate's elbow strengthened. Cade was looking beyond Lisa to Judd, who stood talking with Greg. Judd turned his head and their gazes collided. Cade quickly diverted his attention as though the sight of Judd would transform him into stone.

A hundred impressions crowded Kate's senses. But the one that was foremost was that Cade and Judd were like two powerful warring nations, neither one able to make the first step toward peace.

Cade guided Kate from the banquet room. The silence on the ride to Kate's house was brittle and chilling in the heat of the late-summer day.

The minute her front door shut behind them Cade drew her into his embrace, crushing her against him. When he finally pulled back, holding her face within his hands, his kiss was stormy and devastating. It engulfed her, consumed her, seduced her, nearly destroying any hold she had on sanity.

Kate tried to maintain a semblance of rationality. They had to talk. But when his hands slid away from her face and drifted to her shoulders, then lower to press her hips to his, her pulse hammered wildly beneath his caresses. It was hard for her to think.

When he whispered in a voice rough with longing that he wanted to make love to her, she finally strained away from him.

"Cade, we need to talk."

The circle of his arms trapped her. "Kate, please." All the things he didn't know how to say were embodied in that plea.

But her resolve strengthened. "This won't solve anything, Cade. Tell me what you're feeling."

Her plea fell on deaf ears. His regard formed a tightly aching dryness in her throat. He was shutting her out again and it hurt terribly.

"You want to know what I'm feeling, Kate? I'm feeling sexually frustrated. I want you."

"Damn you, Cade Weston! I let you make love to me once when you were hurting and wouldn't tell me why. I won't do it again." She tried to free herself, but his embrace tightened.

His mouth descended toward hers and Kate twisted her head away. He gripped her chin, forcing her head around. His mouth demanded a response. She tried to reject the rough invasion of her mouth, but he was too strong. She went limp in his arms.

Disgusted with himself, he shoved her away and turned his back on her. His shoulders sagged as he took in deep breaths. "I'm sorry. This wasn't what I'd intended."

"What did you intend, Cade?" Her question betrayed her confusion.

"To make love to you."

"What happened today at the rally?" Kate stepped closer but stopped when she saw him stiffen.

"I had a confrontation with Judd. He wants to be my other investor."

"You don't want him to be."

Cade whirled to face Kate. "You're damn right I don't. He doesn't know what being partners means."

"Judd's a shrewd businessman but he's reasonable, too."

"Don't you defend Judd to me. He's a manipulator and I don't want to be manipulated by him."

Kate took another step toward Cade. "I've told you that my father's very interested in your oil prospect. See him about being your other investor. That would settle your problems."

"No!"

The force of his voice was like a physical blow and Kate backed away. "Why not?"

"Because I'm seeing you."

"What in the world has that got to do with my father?"

"I'll do this on my own, Kate. I won't have people saying I'm dating you for your money."

Rage sizzled through her. "I can't believe what I'm hearing! When in the hell have you cared what other people have thought?"

"The issue is closed, Kate. I will find my own investor if it takes months." Cade braced his feet apart and placed his hands on his hips like a general making sure all his orders were being carried out.

"You're too proud for your own good."

"That's all I have. My pride and self-respect. I have to do this on my own." His face was faintly arrogant.

"Why, Cade? I love you. I want to be a part of your life. Let me in."

He stared at her with a cold, emotionless expression. She was backing him into a corner, demanding things of him he wasn't sure he was capable of giving. He didn't know how to answer her. He had hurt her enough already and had never intended to in the first place.

"Forget it, Cade." Her body slumped in defeat. "I see the answer in your face. Just go and leave me alone."

He hated seeing the despair in her expression but he didn't know how to approach her, tell her what he felt.

"Kate?"

"I love you, Cade, but I have to have something of you to hold on to."

Tears crowded her eyes and escaped down her cheeks. Something died in him as he stared in her eyes, but the words wouldn't get past the lump in his throat. As he walked toward the door, he felt less alive than he ever had in his whole life, but he had nothing to give Kate. She deserved more than he could ever give her, and the best thing for him was to walk away from her and never look back.

When he was seated behind his steering wheel, he finally let go of his emotions. His body quaked; he rested his head on the back of the seat, staring up at the roof with blurred eyes. Kate had been the best thing that ever happened to him, but he wasn't the best thing for her. He had too much of his father in him. He would take the love she had for him and destroy her with it the way Judd had done with his mother. It was better for both of them to cut their losses.

But even as he came to that agonizing decision, he shuddered at the loss of Kate. She had made the last weeks bearable. She had made him smile again.

It was fifteen minutes before Cade could concentrate on his driving. But when he pulled out of the driveway, he'd had no destination in mind. After driving around for an hour he finally stopped in front of Lisa's house. For long moments Cade gazed at the red-brick facade with its charcoal shutters, not really knowing why he was there of all places. He hardly knew Lisa.

But he found himself walking toward Lisa's house, not sure of what he would say to her. All he knew was he didn't want to be alone.

He lifted his hand to ring the doorbell but hesitated before he punched the button. Lisa swung the door open, her surprise wiped from her face by a welcoming smile.

"Cade, what are you doing here?"

"I came to see my sister." He liked the sound of the word "sister."

Lisa stepped aside to let him enter. "Come in. I was just making some dinner. Will you join me?"

"I'm really not hungry, but I'll take a cup of coffee if you have some."

"We can talk in the kitchen."

Cade followed Lisa into the kitchen. "I like your house."

"It needs some work but it's all mine." Lisa put the coffee on, then placed a casserole she had been fixing into the oven before sitting down across from Cade at the kitchen table.

"I'm glad you stopped by, Cade." She glanced away, then back at him. "Dad told me that you two had words at the rally."

"An argument would be a better description, Lisa."

A wry grin touched Lisa's mouth. "I gathered as much. No one has just words with Judd. He has a way of evoking strong emotions in a person."

A question that had been in the back of Cade's mind all his life surfaced. "What was it like growing up with Judd as your father?"

Lisa thought a moment, disturbing memories showing in her disconsolate expression. "I never felt good enough. Judd wanted me to be the boy he couldn't have. He never held me, hugged me or told me he loved me. It hurt like hell because I could never give enough. Judd doesn't show his emotions well."

Cade felt a close bond with his sister. Her description of Judd reinforced his feelings that he was too much like his father. He didn't express his feelings well, either.

"You've learned to accept Judd's lack of emotions?"

"Yes. I used to blame myself for not being the son Judd wanted. I don't anymore. I know Judd is proud of me, but that realization didn't come overnight." Rising, Lisa poured two cups of coffee, then returned to sit across from Cade. "How was it for you?"

"When we grew up most kids had both parents unless one had died. Divorce wasn't very common. And if you only had one parent you stood out, especially if you were a bastard." Cade cradled the warm cup in both hands as he took a sip.

"You were lonely, too," Lisa whispered into the quiet of the kitchen.

"Yes, until I met Jason, Rachel's brother. Then in high school I became a football star and people suddenly forgot my tainted heritage. Or maybe times were starting to change. Who's to say?" Cade shrugged casually as though it meant nothing to him now, but it had left its mark. He had never been able to shake the feeling of being on the outside looking in.

"I was an outsider, too. I was 'Princess Grace' to my classmates and it hurt to hear them talk about me behind my back. They misunderstood my shyness. I finally learned to open up around Kate. With Kate it's hard not to."

Cade laughed, but the sound was hollow. "She does have that effect on people."

Lisa looked pointedly at him. "She deserves the best."

"And what are my intentions? The best, Lisa. I'm walking away from her."

"Why?"

"You can sit there and ask that after you've lived with Judd and suffered because he wouldn't tell you he loved you? Just look at our mothers." Cade downed the coffee in several gulps, then walked to the counter to pour some more.

"You're not Judd."

"I have our father's blood," Cade replied bitterly as he sat again.

Lisa reached across the table and laid her hand over his. "You don't have to be like that. Talk with Judd, Cade. He's changed. Since his heart attack he's looking at life differently. I don't think he feels so invincible anymore. Finally he and Mother are truly married."

Cade tensed, but he didn't pull his hand away. "All I see is a man who's trying to worm his way into my life and take it over."

"You two are like two rams who butt their heads together to try to prove who's superior." Lisa shook her head and took a sip of her coffee. "Stubbornness is definitely a Masters trait."

"How did the rally go?" he asked to change the subject.

"I left right after you did." Her face clouded.

"What happened?"

Lisa trailed her fingertip around the rim of her cup, staring into the brown liquid. "Judd seems to think Greg and I would make a nice couple. I left before he could put that plan into action."

"I see he likes to manipulate your life, too. We'll have to compare notes sometime."

"Yes, he's certainly done his share. Tell me about my nephew."

Cade brightened. "Matthew is wonderful. He's a great kid."

"Maybe his father's blood flows strongly in his veins," Lisa teased.

But Cade paled and murmured, "Possibly."

"What's wrong?" Lisa wrinkled her brow in confusion.

"Nothing." Cade grinned, but the proud sheen in his dark eyes had dulled.

"I'd like to get to know him. Maybe he'd like to come out to the ranch to go riding. Does he like horses?"

"Are you kidding! He'd jump at the chance to ride a horse." He paused, then continued, "Lisa, I haven't told him who my father is, but I think it's about time that I do. I would like him to get to know you."

"What about Judd? You know he won't be able to walk away from a grandson now that everything is out in the open. He kept quiet because of Mother and me."

Cade drew in a deep breath, then exhaled slowly. "I don't know. My first reaction is to say no. But for some reason I'm not sure if that's fair."

"Well, we have plenty of time."

"Speaking of time, I think I'd better be going."

"Please stay for dinner, Cade. I hate eating alone."

The word "alone" was what changed Cade's mind. He didn't like eating alone, either. "Okay."

While Lisa and Cade ate dinner they discussed his oil prospect and Masters Corporation. By the time they finished dinner they were completely comfortable and relaxed with each other.

"I really do need to go now, Lisa." Cade stood and took his dishes to the sink.

Lisa walked him to the front door. "Cade, have you ever thought that maybe you are the best thing for Kate?"

Cade didn't say anything as he turned to leave. Then suddenly he swung around and gathered Lisa to him in a fierce hug. "I'm glad we talked, Lisa."

"So am I."

Cade left his sister with one part of his life resolved. But her question plagued him on the long drive to his house. When he let himself in, memories of embracing Kate in the living room earlier that day assailed him. It seemed a lifetime ago.

Cade walked to the phone and punched Kate's first two numbers.

What do I have to offer her?

He slowly pressed down the third number, his finger lingering on the button.

Nothing.

He replaced the receiver quietly.

Chapter Ten

Kate paced restlessly across the floor of her office. Despite the fact she wore a jacket, she was cold. Clayton Simon had asked to see her before the board meeting to give her the decision on who would be the next president of the Denver Exchange Bank.

But that wasn't what made her feel so cold inside. For the past two weeks she had tried to take each day as it came, but she felt empty. When Cade had walked out of her house the night of the rally, he had taken part of her with him. The hollow sensation in the pit of her stomach hadn't subsided over the past weeks.

She had to get on with her life. The presidency was even more important to her now because the job would require her complete concentration. She knew she was qualified and was capable of handling the job, but Samuel was stiff competition.

The knocking sound at the door held her immobile. She turned toward it, fighting to keep the dread she felt from her expression as Clayton Simon entered her office.

Kate crossed the room and shook his hand. "It's good to see you, Clayton."

When they were both seated, Clayton immediately started, "Kate, my family and I are very grateful for all you've done since Dad's death. I've had my hands full with my own company and trying to bring some kind of order to Dad's estate." He cleared his throat, shifting in the chair. "We only have a few minutes before the board meeting, but I wanted to speak with you privately beforehand. I know how much you wanted the presidency, and your being a woman, I didn't..." His voice trailed off into silence, as though he didn't need to complete the sentence.

Kate understood what he meant by that unfinished remark: being a woman she might create an emotional scene that would upset the board members, all men. Clayton was certainly not like his father.

Bristling with anger, she sat perfectly still, her mind numb as she listened to Clayton explain his decision.

"You both have the same record at the bank, but Samuel has more years of experience. I wanted you to know your position at the bank is still yours. You're a valuable asset to us. I'll remain chairman of the board to keep tabs on everything."

Kate heard the words, and their meaning even registered in her mind, but she felt as if she was observing the scene from afar.

Standing abruptly, he added, "You'll have complete freedom within your department, Kate. I have faith in your ability and don't want to lose you."

"I appreciate your telling me beforehand. Thank you for your vote of confidence," she said in a formal, polite tone.

Kate walked Clayton calmly to the door, but when it closed behind him, her legs were trembling so much that she had to sag against the door for support. That job had been the answer to some of her problems, but now, instead, she would be working for Samuel. She fumed at that thought and decided to send letters to banks in other parts of the country. She had nothing to keep her in Denver now. She couldn't handle running into Cade.

When her private line rang, Kate jumped, startled from her thoughts. She hurried to answer it.

"Hi, Kate, this is Lisa. I just wanted to know if you'd like to go see *Winter's Repast*. It's closing tonight and the reviews have been great."

Suspicion crossed Kate's face. She could tell by her friend's tone of voice that there was more to the invitation than simply seeing a play. "Lisa Masters, this invitation wouldn't have anything to do with the fact that Cade's mother is involved with the play, would it? Because if it does, I have to tell you it's over between Cade and me."

"Do you want it to be?"

"Yes. No. But I've done everything humanly possible where Cade Weston is concerned," Kate said in a choked voice. The past month had been difficult. She felt as though her whole life was falling apart. "I think it's best I don't go with you tonight."

"Are you sure you won't go?"

"Yes, I'm sure." Her control was slipping quickly. "Listen, Lisa, there's a meeting in five minutes. Have a nice time tonight."

Kate's hand lingered on the receiver after she hung up. She started to dial Cade's number. She needed him badly right now. She was hurting and he was the only one who could soothe that hurt.

But she had done everything to get Cade to love her, and he didn't. It was that simple. There was nothing else she could do. Kate took her hand off the receiver and rose to leave her office, her cool professional facade in place.

"Mom, what are you doing here?" Cade asked, surprised to see his mother at his front door. She should be at the theater.

"Are you alone?" Ruth asked.

His mother's unusually pale face alarmed him. "Mother? Are you all right?"

"Is anyone here?"

The urgency in her voice heightened his apprehension. "Matthew's getting dressed for tonight."

"I've been trying to reach you. I need to talk to you." Ruth moved past Cade into the living room.

Cade stood motionless in the doorway, watching her prowl around the room, skittish as an unbroken filly. Finally he sat, waiting for his mother to speak.

Ruth halted in the middle of the room, running her hand restlessly along the strap of her purse. "I'm not particularly proud of what I have to tell you, Cade. Since that scene between you and Judd at my house, I've been thinking a lot about what I did years ago."

Cade started to speak but she waved him quiet. "No, please hear me out. Judd wanted to come see you, but I wouldn't let him. It was my fault, Cade."

Cade shot to his feet, furious. "No! Don't protect that man anymore. Haven't you shouldered enough all these years?"

Sorrow lined her features; distress darkened her eyes. "Judd wanted to see you, Cade, but I couldn't handle the situation. I tried, but I just couldn't." Her eyelids squeezed shut for an agonizing moment as she continued in a hoarse voice, "Please forgive me." Tears spilled from behind her eyelids and streaked down her cheeks.

Cade couldn't move. He didn't want to hear her defending Judd. He was still hurting her, even after thirty-five years. Judd had had a choice. He was to blame.

Ruth opened her glistening eyes and stared at Cade beseechingly. "The only defense I can give you is that I didn't realize what I was doing to you. I couldn't see beyond my own hurt to see yours. When I finally did see it, the damage had been done and I didn't know how to approach you. That scene at my house made me realize I had to stop running away. I knew I had to tell you everything, even if I lost your respect and love." She appeared fragile, yet strong; someone caught in a moment of human weakness.

Numb, Cade couldn't think of anything to say. He didn't want to think about Judd. He was still the man who tried to run his life and who could have seen his son if he had really wanted to. Ruth's revelation didn't change that fact.

"Your father loves you, Cade. Give him a chance. I'm the one you should be angry at."

The tears choking her voice propelled Cade forward. He drew his mother into his arms and held her tightly. His mind was speeding so fast, trying to cling to a rational, sane thought, but in those few minutes of silence Cade felt sanity was just out of reach. He knew it would take time to sort through everything and digest what his mother had revealed.

He focused on one thing, to comfort his mother, to protect her from further suffering. "Mom, I love you. That will never change. You always gave me your love and attention unselfishly. I can't forget that, and what you said won't alter it."

"Dad, I'm ready to go." Matthew stopped in the doorway when he saw his grandmother.

Cade and Ruth parted. Ruth turned away for a moment to compose herself before she faced her grandson. She smiled, but sadness was still evident in her eyes. She was fighting desperately to conceal it from Matthew.

"Grandma?" Matthew hesitated, uncertain. "Are you riding with us to the theater?" His glance moved quickly from his grandmother to his father, then back.

When Ruth answered him, her voice was even. "No, I just stopped by for a minute. I wanted to make sure you'd both be coming to the party afterward." She glanced down at her watch, her movements jerky. "In fact, if I don't get going Paul will have my head." She kissed Cade, a silent message of love and thanks, then hugged Matthew and kissed him. "You're going to help me, aren't you?"

"Oh, yes, Grandma. I love working backstage."

"Then I'll see you in a little bit."

Wordlessly Cade walked with Ruth out to her car. When she was seated behind the wheel, she rolled down her window.

"I never told you this, but I always felt I was the luckiest kid around to have you for a mother."

The tears returned to her eyes as she covered his hand with hers. "Judd doesn't have a lot of finesse when it comes to expressing his feelings. He did it for me, Cade. Think about that."

"I will, Mom."

Cade watched his mother drive away. His iron control was restored, but the cost had been great to his emotions. His mother's revelation made him realize he had a few things to clear up with Matthew.

Matthew was sitting on the couch, dressed in the one suit he hadn't outgrown. Laughing, Cade shook his head in astonishment.

"I can't believe it, Matthew. You're growing so fast it will take a fortune to keep you in clothes."

"I'm only taking after you. I want to be as tall as you, so I can play football like you did."

Nervous, Cade sat across from Matthew. Cade had been avoiding the subject for the past two weeks, but he couldn't postpone it any longer. Lisa would be at the play and probably at the cast party.

"Matthew, I need to talk with you before we go to the play." Cade ran his fingers through his hair.

"Dad, is it about Kate?"

The thought of Kate and their last meeting brought a frown to Cade's features. His life had been hell since then. He hadn't realized how much Kate had been in his life. "No, son. It's about your grandfather."

"Grandfather Hawke? Has something happened to him?" Panic laced Matthew's voice.

"No. *My* father, Matthew." Cade clasped his hands tightly together in front of him. Lord, this wasn't easy.

"But you don't have a father."

"I know you think my father is dead, but he isn't. He lives just outside of Denver."

Matthew's face screwed into a look of puzzlement and Cade hastened to explain, "Your grandmother never married my father and he has another family. We haven't said anything until now because he didn't want to hurt his other family."

Matthew thought that over for a minute, then asked, "Do I have any cousins?"

"No, but you have an aunt who would love to get to know you."

"Who?"

"Lisa Masters. Judd Masters is my father." Strangely, saying it relieved Cade immensely. It was finally out in the open, no longer a secret to be guarded. It still wasn't common knowledge, but the people he cared about the most knew the real facts.

Matthew tilted his head to one side and asked, "Isn't she the one I met at the rally?"

Cade nodded. "She's coming tonight to the play. I must also tell you, son, that a lot of people don't know about my relationship with Judd. He's a powerful man in Colorado and I don't want this to come out unless it comes from him. Do you understand?" Listening to himself explain in a calm, rational voice made Cade feel strange. He always felt intensely emotional when he thought about Judd, but for some reason the emotions just weren't there at the moment.

Matthew's adult expression appeared on his face. "I won't say anything, Dad."

"Good. Now we'd better go. I don't want to miss this play."

When they stood to leave Cade ruffled his son's hair affectionately, then embraced him. Matthew would never experience not being hugged or told he was loved by his father.

On the ride to the theater, Matthew said, "Do you know, Dad, that Grandma's been going out with Mr. Carson?"

Cade nearly swerved off the expressway. "She's been dating? Who told you?"

"She did. You ought to see Grandma when she's around Mr. Carson at the theater."

"Mr. Carson is the director?"

"Yeah. He teaches at the university and he's a writer, too. I think Grandma really likes him. He's a nice man and always talks to me."

Except for his mother's brief visit a while ago, Cade hadn't been by to see her because he had been trying to find his second investor. In fact, he'd just returned from a trip to Dallas and Houston late the night before. He'd been thankful for the diversion from thinking about Kate, but it lasted only until nighttime. Then his dreams about Kate started. Damn, he felt possessed by her.

"Well, if your grandmother likes him, then he must be pretty nice." Cade parked his truck next to the theater.

They arrived early, so Matthew could help backstage. His son had seen the play every night, but this was Cade's first time. He was too restless to sit in his seat, so he wandered around the lobby. Lisa was meeting him soon.

He refused to think about what his mother had told him. It was still too new, so he busied himself by watching people enter the theater. A crowd was gathering when Cade spotted Lisa, and he waved her over to him.

"I'm sorry I'm late. Something came up at work that needed my immediate attention. We're planning a shopping center in southeast Denver that's running into some snags. But with a project that big it's to be expected."

Cade handed their tickets to the usher and escorted Lisa to their seats. "Has Judd given you free rein?"

Lisa laughed. "As much as Judd can. Right now he and Mother are out of town on vacation, if you can believe that."

"That is hard to believe. A business trip maybe, but a vacation, that's a shock." That was the third piece of unexpected news in the past hour. His mind was having a hard time assimilating it all.

The curtain opened, and Cade forced his thoughts away from his problems to enjoy the play.

When the play ended and the audience was leaving, Cade said to Lisa, "I hope you'll come to the party afterward."

"I wish I could, but it's been a very long day and tomorrow promises to be even longer." Lisa started to say something else but didn't.

Cade stopped and pulled her out of the rush of people. "I wanted you to know that I told Matthew about you and Judd. He's intrigued with the idea that he has an aunt and grandfather but disappointed he doesn't have any cousins. You're going to have to work on that one, Lisa."

A playfulness twinkled in Lisa's eyes. "You could always give him a brother or sister."

"That's not likely. I can barely support myself, let alone a wife and children." A closed look fell into place, communicating clearly that the subject was off limits.

In silence they wove their way through the crowd to the steps that led backstage. Ruth was standing next to the director, her dark features alive with a smile, her eyes bright.

"Lisa, Cade, this is Paul Carson."

While his mother made the introductions, Cade's attention was totally on her. She looked different. A spirited spark animated her quiet beauty, which spurred Cade's curiosity even more about the director. Cade had honestly thought that he would never see that look because of Judd.

"I had to tell you that the play was wonderful. And, Ms. Weston, the costumes were lovely. They fit the story so well," Lisa said with a smile that held a tinge of strain.

"Please call me Ruth."

Cade could tell Lisa was nervous, but his mother talked with her, putting her at ease. While they conversed, Cade assessed Paul Carson. The man had to be about the same age as Ruth and he kept himself in good shape. There was an air of dignity about him that Cade liked.

Lisa drew Cade into the conversation, asking where he'd been all week. "I've been out of town trying to find that last investor. I think I'll start going through the phone book and calling perfect strangers."

"Ruth told me about your oil prospect," Paul said, his hazel eyes now doing the gauging. "I have some money to invest. Why don't you come by the house tomorrow afternoon and we'll discuss it?"

Cade hid his surprise behind a bland expression. He hadn't realized the director had that much money. Maybe Paul Carson didn't know how much it would take to invest. "You would have to put up one hundred thousand dollars."

"That seems reasonable. I've looked into oil prospects before."

The light in Paul's eyes told Cade that the other man had known exactly what Cade would think. "Fine. How about two o'clock then?"

"Dad, what did you think?" Matthew came bounding up to the group. "I helped with the scenery."

"You did a fantastic job, Matthew. Son, you remember Lisa Masters."

"Yes." Matthew smiled shyly up at her.

"I hope I can persuade you to come out to the ranch one day to go riding. I heard you love horses."

"Oh, yes!"

"Then I'll call you and we'll set up a time for next weekend. How's that, Matthew?"

"Great!"

"We'd better be going, Ruth," Paul interrupted. "I want to make sure everything is set up before hordes of hungry actors descend on my modest abode."

"Modest, indeed! Your house has at least fifteen rooms," Ruth teased, slipping her arm through Paul's. "I'm not sure if it's your money or your talent that's more intriguing."

Paul laughed, a robust, rich sound. "How about both?"

"I'm going with Grandma, Dad." Matthew quickly followed the pair, leaving Lisa and Cade alone.

Cade leaned back against the wall with his arms casually folded across his chest. "I somehow have the impression you want to tell me something. What's wrong, Lisa?"

"We're a lot alike, aren't we?"

"Yes, and you're avoiding my question."

"All evening I've been wondering if I should tell you. Denver Exchange Bank has a new president."

"Who?" Cade straightened, alert; his question held the urgency that he felt.

"Samuel Coleman."

Kate lost. She must be going through hell right now. She had wanted that job, and to lose to Samuel must have been hard to take. Cade had the strong urge to see her, to hold her and give her comfort. She needed him tonight and he wasn't going to let her down.

Cade was out the stage door when he tossed over his shoulder, "Thanks, Lisa. I'm glad you told me."

The urgency increased with each step. All he knew was that he couldn't let Kate go through this alone. He didn't think beyond that.

It didn't take Cade more than fifteen minutes to get to Kate's house. When he rang her doorbell, there was no hesitation. All his concerns converged on Kate and her despondency.

When Kate opened the door, Cade was transfixed by the desolate look in her eyes that she vainly tried to mask. His heart stopped beating for a few seconds as he lifted his hand toward her.

She shrank away from his touch. "No, Cade. Please leave." Her voice caught. "I can't handle it right now."

His hand fell back to his side, but he didn't leave. "I'm not going, Kate." There was a firm resolve in his voice.

"My emotions have been taking a beating lately." Her eyes glistened with unshed tears. "Please."

"You need me, Kate."

"I need your love, Cade." A lone tear escaped and cascaded down her cheek. She wiped furiously at it as she backed away, but her tears shimmered.

Cade entered and kicked the door closed. The sound halted Kate and she stood frozen, another tear leaving a wet trail on her face.

He gathered her against him, cradling her head on his shoulder. "Cry if you need to, darling," Cade whispered against her hair as he stroked it. "I'm here for you."

The sobs that had been locked away since Cade's departure two weeks before racked her body. Her love for him was stronger than her pride. She realized she would take him on any terms because her life was meaningless without him. Her tears were more for what was out of reach than for the presidency she had lost.

When she could no longer cry, she noticed that his comforting strokes were changing to caresses that were awakening her body. She nestled closer, the staccato beat of his heart testifying to her effect on him. He might not love her, but he wanted her. Maybe that would be enough, Kate thought briefly before Cade swung her up into his arms and headed for her bedroom.

He laid her gently on the bed, then impatiently stripped off his clothes, his eyes never leaving her face. Kneeling down on the bed beside her, he untied her robe, parting the terry material. Underneath she wore only a cream-colored satin teddy.

Cade stared down at her, drawing in his breath sharply. He had never seen a more beautiful woman, he thought as he pushed her robe off her shoulders. The flimsy teddy was so sexy that he shuddered with anticipation. His hands shook as he removed the last wisp of clothing to reveal the smooth silkiness of her skin to his fevered gaze.

His eyes spoke silent messages as they roamed over her. "You're so special, Kate. I haven't been able to get you out of my mind. You have me completely bewitched."

The soft cadence of his voice washed away her suffering and sparked her hope. Perhaps in time he would love her.

He stretched out beside her, his mouth nibbling the ultrasensitive flesh of her throat. Then his lips were parting hers, opening them. From that moment on she was completely lost to the glorious promise of his lips and hands, to his whispered eroticism that filled the stillness of the night. Explosions of pleasure erased everything from her mind except Cade. Her heart and soul would always be his.

Afterward in the darkness they lay side by side, her head resting in the nook of his shoulder. She drew lazy circles on his chest, her fingers tangling in the patch of dark-blond hair.

"Kate, for the first time I felt you needed me."

Her head shot up and she gazed at his darkened profile. "I've always needed you."

"Not really. You're a very strong woman, Kate Dole."

She sensed the sardonic slant of his mouth. "I love you, Cade."

"Loving a person and needing them are two different things."

He paused and Kate felt he had something else on his mind. She waited, hoping he would share it with her.

"Kate, I can't give you any promises. I don't love easily, but the feelings I have for you scare the hell out of me."

"I'm a very patient woman, Cade."

"I can't offer you anything until I see what happens to my oil prospect. I'm not even sure I have my last investor. My future is very uncertain and I won't ask someone to share that with me."

"Cade, I would share anything with you." She bent over and mated her lips to his, pushing her tongue into the cavity of his mouth.

"There is so much I want to give you, but the waiting may be a lifetime, Kate," he murmured against her lips.

The throbbing ache in her heart momentarily overwhelmed her. Her whole future hung in the balance. Cade wouldn't allow himself to think about the future beyond his first oil well. All she could offer him was emotional support and the prayer that soon his well would come in. Her happiness hinged on that.

Chapter Eleven

Kate rushed to answer the front door, and when she opened it she was in Cade's arms before he had time to say hello. Laughing, he swung her around and planted a firm kiss on her mouth.

"I like that kind of greeting," he murmured, and sampled her lips over and over.

"I didn't even check to make sure it was you."

"I don't like the idea some other guy could have received that welcome."

"Jealous?"

"Absolutely, woman," he growled in her ear as he backed her into her house. He pushed the door closed with his booted foot and drew her up against him. "Mmm. You smell so much nicer than an oil rig. Your perfume drives me crazy. All I could think of out at the rig was that scent and you without..." His dark eyes smoked, silently imparting the rest of the sentence.

"Well, thank you for the compliment, but I'm not so sure I like being compared to oil, even if it's favorably."

"Could we skip your dad's birthday party?" He breathed the last word against her slightly parted lips.

"We'll have plenty of time later, Cade." Her voice quavered with her own desires. "I wasn't sure you'd make it. I'm glad you did."

"I told you I would if we weren't ready to perforate the drilling pipe. I want to be there for the big moment, so I'll have to leave early tomorrow morning."

Kate tilted her head back and saw the eagerness in his expression. "May I come, Cade?"

"I have to leave at five. It could be all day or longer."

"Do you think that would stop me? I usually wake up at six anyway. I don't want to miss this. If I stay in Denver I'll go crazy with curiosity."

He kissed the tip of her nose. "Yes, I know about your curiosity. Okay, you can come."

"How is the well?" She was almost afraid to ask. She hadn't seen much of Cade since they had logged the well and run pipe down the hole. He had been at the site most of the time during that critical period.

"Except for when that wrench was dropped into the hole and it took three days to fish it out, we've had little trouble. I feel like an expectant father waiting for his child to be born. The log looked good." His eyes glowed with enthusiasm that he could barely contain. "But, of course, you can never really tell until we perforate," Cade added, trying to temper his zeal. "The log is just an indicator. It's still a guessing game."

"Then what's your guess?"

"Of course I think there's oil down there or I wouldn't have given the okay for the pipe. That's an extra fifty thousand dollars, so I'm banking the log proves right."

"It doesn't always?"

Cade shook his head, moving farther into the living room to sit on the couch. "Kate, I've seen bad logs that made terrific wells and I've seen the reverse."

"Oh." She sank down next to him, taking his hand in hers. "What happens if the well is dry, Cade?" The question barely got past the lump in her throat.

He sucked in a deep breath and squeezed her fingers. "Let's pray it isn't, but if it is, then I'll go back to Howard and Paul and ask for more money to drill a second well. There's oil under the ground out there. I just hope I picked the right place."

"Will they give it to you?" Her heart was pounding; her palms were sweaty.

"I hope so. They'll be mad as hell, but they already sank a lot of money into this project." He paused, his thumb rubbing circles in the palm of her hand. "If I have to drill a second well, Kate, my share will be less because I don't have a hundred thousand to put up. Howard and Paul will have to carry more of the obligation or I'll have to find another investor to make up the fifty thousand I'll be short."

She was used to large amounts of money being discussed, but sitting next to Cade and talking about thousands of dollars panicked her. It was his money, not a stranger's, they were discussing. If he drilled a second well, he would use up all his credit. If both wells were dry, that would be the end of his dream, and hers. The pounding in her heart accelerated. She was scared.

"I could put up the fifty thousand, Cade. Thomas's insurance money is just sitting there drawing interest. I want you to use it if you have to."

Kate felt the tension in Cade, communicated through the death grip on her hand.

"We've already been through this before, Kate. It doesn't make any difference if it's your money or your father's." His voice was tautly controlled as he relinquished his grip on her hand.

Kate's own sudden anger boiled to the surface. "When are you going to stop letting your damn pride stand in the way of good business sense? What's wrong with me giving you the money?"

Cade took her face in his hands and said, "I have to do it my way, Kate. I love you. It's important for me not to accept any money from you or your family. You'll have to trust me."

Her mind went blank. Cade loved her! It took a stunned moment for her to assemble her thoughts. There were still some things that needed to be said.

"It works both ways, Cade." She covered his hands with her own, trying to restrain the wild thrilling sensations that were clamoring for release. It took supreme willpower to say in a level voice, "You say you love me, but do you trust me with your feelings? I want to be a part of your life. I want to know what you're thinking and feeling."

His mouth tilted roguishly. "I'm feeling extremely lucky to have found you. I'm also feeling frustrated that we have to leave in a few minutes."

"Are you being evasive?" The question was serious, but she couldn't help the smile.

"Not evasive, just truthful. I am a lucky man. Believe that, Kathleen Dole." He touched her lips softly with his. "But your parents are expecting us. I wouldn't want to arouse the wrath of the Stanfields."

"And you'd better remember that when you have a lustful thought," she teased, her excitement evident in her expression.

"What about when you have a lustful thought?"

"Me?"

Amusement crinkled the lines at the corners of his eyes. "Yes, you."

"You'd better look out." She was on her feet and across the room before she had finished speaking.

Cade's laughter warmed her. It had been a month since the night of the play's closing and they had spent every spare moment together. Often Matthew would join them for an outing, and Kate especially liked those times because it seemed as though they were a family.

As they walked to Cade's truck, he asked, "How old is your father today?"

"Sixty."

"Do we mention it?"

"He'll probably say something about it. As far as he's concerned, he's not a day over thirty-five."

"Your father is quite a character." Cade backed his truck out of the parking space.

"Yes. No matter how busy he was when we were growing up he always had time for us. I remember once Dad refused to speak at an important political rally because I was in the school play. I didn't even have the lead, but he was there."

Kate looked sideways at him, suddenly regretting her journey into the past because of Cade's longing to have a father. "Cade, I didn't mean..."

"No, that's okay." It had been a month since his mother had told him about her not allowing his father to visit them. *His father.* He had thought of the man as "Judd" for so long that it was hard to change, and he wasn't even sure he wanted to. Judd was still Judd, a domineering man who liked to control. Cade still found himself confused, and until he knew what his feelings were he intended to avoid his father. He was afraid he would widen the gap between them.

Cade added with a wistful smile, "You can't guard your every word concerning your father, Kate. You love him and I won't ask you not to say anything about him. He's a good man, well respected by even his opponents."

"Dad has opponents?" Kate asked in mock seriousness, trying to lighten the atmosphere.

Cade chuckled softly. "Not many, but a few."

"Well, let's not tell him. I wouldn't want to spoil his birthday party."

Cade parked the truck. "Wild horses couldn't drag the truth out of me."

They were laughing when Greg opened the front door. As they walked into the house, the more they tried to contain their laughter the more they laughed.

"Is it a private joke or can you share it with the rest of us?" Greg asked, sending them both strange looks.

"I swore I wouldn't say a word on pain of death." Cade shook Greg's hand, then placed his arm around Kate's shoulders as they all made their way into the living room.

Everyone was already there, and after Cade and Kate exchanged greetings with the rest of the Stanfield family, the talk turned to Greg's campaign and his uphill battle for victory.

While Kate's father opened his presents, Cade relaxed back on the couch with Kate next to him. Occasionally the fragrance of her perfume wafted to him, and he resisted the strong urge to kiss her in front of her family. Instead, he enjoyed the camaraderie among the Stanfields.

Kate was helping him to fill an emptiness in his life. With her he realized even more the importance of family, and that realization had given him the courage to approach Lisa. During the past month he and Lisa had seen each other several times, and their relationship was becoming a comfortable one. Cade was in Kate's debt for more reasons than one.

Until he had spoken the words earlier to Kate, he hadn't realized the depth of his feelings toward her. He loved her. If everything went all right at the rig, he would ask her to marry him tomorrow night. He wanted to share his life with her.

Kate and Cade were the first ones to leave. The minute the front door closed behind them Cade hauled her against him and kissed her hard on the lips.

"I've been wanting to do that all evening, Kate. If we'd stayed much longer, I would have shocked your family."

"Why are we standing out here?"

Cade had to restrain himself from speeding through the streets of Denver. His hands tapped impatiently on the steering wheel when he was forced to sit at a stoplight. Fifteen minutes later, they arrived at Kate's house.

They were just inside the front door when Cade pulled Kate to him, his fingers fumbling with the buttons of her shirt. "Woman, I think you wore this shirt to frustrate me. There must be at least ten buttons."

When he removed her shirt, his eyes boldly feasted upon her breasts, half-covered with a lacy bra. Kate's sweater and purse slipped to the floor as she watched him look at her.

Because they had hours to savor each other, Cade was no longer in a rush. He lifted her hand to his mouth and nibbled on the tips of each finger, their eye contact strong and unbroken.

"This was the rest of my dream. I wanted to undress you slowly and explore every part of you."

"We certainly have a lot in common. That was the very same dream I had."

He unsnapped her bra and it fell to the floor. Leaning forward, he flicked his tongue over her hardened nipples. He crushed her against him and whispered into her ear, "I love you, Kate. When I need you, you're there. I want to give you the world."

"I don't want the world, Cade. Only you," she murmured against his chest.

His mouth feathered along her throat, nipping at the sensitive skin as he whispered all the things he wanted to do to her. His lips covered hers with smothering force, and his tongue examined the soft interior of her mouth, boldly caressing hers.

He lowered his head to suckle her breast, moving from one to the other. Lightning sensations tingled through her and she shuddered with excitement. She dug her hands into his shoulders as his lips traveled even lower. Unfastening her pants, he slid them down over her hips, and his tongue lazily circled her navel while he removed the rest of her clothes. His hands kneaded and massaged as his mouth brushed, teased and tasted her.

She was sure her knees would buckle if Cade weren't holding her up. Kate urged him to his feet and leisurely undressed him, her hands dancing lightly over his muscled body with enticing sureness. Beneath her fingertips she felt his trembling reaction.

When they stood naked, facing each other, Kate drew Cade into the living room, where they sank to the plush carpet. The first time they came together in an urgent mating, wildly frenzied. The second time in Kate's brass bed it was a slow, tender exploration. Their union was the consummation of love.

Much later Cade sat propped up against the headboard, cradling Kate against him, absently stroking her. For comfortable, peaceful moments silence reigned.

It wasn't broken until Cade said, "I want to tell you about my marriage, Kate."

"You don't have to, Cade." The suddenly very sober tone in his voice alarmed her.

"I have to. I want you to understand me and yet I haven't told you a lot about myself. When Rachel and I married, it was for different reasons than most people's." He paused, drawing in a deep breath as he tightly embraced her. "Matthew isn't my son. In fact, the main reason we married was that Rachel was pregnant."

"Then you knew about the baby when you married her?" His arm was a band around her, communicating feelings he hadn't shared with anyone else.

"We grew up together. Her brother was my best friend and Rachel and I were good friends, too. She needed a friend desperately then."

The vehemence in Cade's voice told Kate a lot. Cade didn't call someone a friend lightly, and when he gave his friendship it was a gift for life.

Kate angled herself to look up into his face. The faraway expression in his eyes spoke of the memories he was reliving. Then, as if sensing she was staring at him, he smiled faintly down at her.

The reassuring smile was a brief flash before he continued, "I couldn't let Rachel and her baby go through what my mother and I did. Matthew will always have a father. I will always be there for him."

In his eyes Kate could see the intense emotions he kept locked away from the world, and she respected the silence that followed. She needed time to digest all that Cade was telling her. He might not be Matthew's biological father, but he was Matthew's father in every other sense.

When Cade looked back at Kate, his eyes were clouded, his usual control elusive. "Rachel and I hadn't intended to stay married long. But after Matthew was born, one year became two, then three. We had a quiet, peaceful home life and Matthew grew up in a house full of love. I loved Rachel, and when she died I was alone again, even though I had Matthew." His hold on Kate strengthened, as though he was afraid to let go. "I didn't like that feeling, Kate, but I learned to live with it until you came along and showed me how lonely life can be without someone to love."

Cade continued to speak about his childhood, his determination that his son would never know the shame of being illegitimate, of his fear that one day he might lose Matthew to his real father, even though Cade knew that wasn't possible. Silent tears filled Kate's eyes and spilled over to run down her cheeks. He was opening up to her and telling her of the pain he had been carrying around deep inside. He was sharing a part of himself he didn't share, and she treasured the moment.

When he saw her tears, his mouth quivered with a smile. "Don't cry for me, Kate. I'm only telling you this so you'll understand why I learned to be a loner."

"I'm not crying for you but for the little boy who was hurt terribly and kept it inside himself." Kate sat up and knelt next to Cade, facing him. "I love you, darling. I know it wasn't easy for you to tell me. But I know you trust me as well as love me."

With his thumbs he caressed away all traces of her tears. "Thank you for caring enough to listen." He pulled her head toward him and kissed each eyelid. "If we intend to be up at five, we'd better at least get a few hours of sleep," he whispered against her forehead.

Nestled against Cade's warmth, Kate's eyelids drifted closed. Somehow everything would work out because she didn't intend for Cade ever to be alone again.

At the well site Kate slipped into her light jacket. The October day was crisp and refreshing as she took in Cade's operation. The rig jutted upward seventy feet, hard and angular against the softness of the blue sky. It reminded Kate of Cade, a man who was reaching toward the sky with his dream. The softness was hidden beneath his tough veneer.

Cade seemed to forget her presence as he walked toward a man wearing a hard hat. The tall, rangy-built man with sun-streaked hair pointed toward her and Cade turned, motioning her over to them.

Thrusting a hard hat into her hand, Cade introduced Kate to Jim Bary, the tool pusher. Jim had a scowl on his face that seemed to be permanently etched there. His eyes, harsh, were piercing as they looked her over.

Cade's question diverted Jim Bary's attention away from her. "Are we ready to perforate the well?"

"The crew has just finished rigging up."

"I'll grab a cup of coffee and meet you in the perforating truck." Cade took Kate's elbow and guided her toward a trailer set away from the rig.

Inside, Kate scanned the room that was obviously used as a rest area with several cots along the walls, a work place and a cafeteria for the roughnecks. When she faced Cade she suddenly felt like an outsider. This was a whole different world, a dangerous one.

"What happens after you perforate the well?" She felt helpless. Maybe she shouldn't have come. All she could do was wait and watch.

"If we're lucky, the well will flow. If we're not and there's no response after we perforate, then we'll swab on it for a little while."

Kate watched him pour some coffee into a Styrofoam cup. Outwardly he appeared calm and in complete control of himself, while she was tied up in knots and didn't think she could even drink a cup of coffee.

Cade placed his cup on a table and drew her tightly against him. "I think it would be better for you to stay in here. The perforating truck will be cramped and there isn't any room on the floor of a completion rig for more than one or two people. I'll keep you posted, Kate. If we're lucky, I won't be too long."

The only indication of the pressure he was feeling was in his impassioned hug. As he left the trailer she called out, "Good luck."

A quicksilver smile flashed into his eyes before the door closed.

She didn't move from the window for two hours. She refused to think of anything. She just watched and waited, occasionally catching a glimpse of Cade at the rig site. It wasn't until she saw Jim Bary coming toward the trailer that she moved away. With her hands in her pockets to conceal their trembling, she swung toward the door as it opened.

"Cade's busy, but he wanted you to know there was no response, so they're swabbing on the well now." Jim walked to the coffeepot and poured himself a cup.

"For how long?" she asked, aware of the animosity in the tool pusher's expression.

"Two or three hours."

"Then what?"

"If we don't get anything, we'll shut in overnight and hope the pressure builds up, then we'll acidize first thing tomorrow morning."

Chilled, Kate rubbed her hands together as though to warm them. "Does the acid usually work?"

"About a third of the time," he answered crisply, downing his coffee in several gulps.

When Jim returned to the rig floor, the lonely waiting began again. By the time Cade was striding toward the trailer, Kate had worn a path from the window to the stove. She finally drank one cup of coffee, then two, then three. Her nerves were raw as the door was thrust open and Cade stood framed in the doorway.

She froze. The look on his face answered her silent question. There had been no response with the swabbing. There was only one more hope and they would have to wait overnight until the next morning to know if that worked.

"I'll drive you back to Denver," Cade said wearily, removing his hard hat and placing it on the table next to the one she had brought into the trailer hours before.

"What are you going to do after that?" Her eyes were glued to the hard hats, a symbol of the danger involved in drilling for oil. But there was more than just physical danger. During the long wait her nerves had taken a beating.

"Turn around and come back."

"Then I'm staying here." There was impregnable steel in her voice.

"Kate," he sighed her name, "I won't be much company. Too much on my mind."

"I know. I just want to be with you."

"Then I'll get a motel room in town. I doubt I'll do much sleeping, but there's no sense both of us being worn out."

They ate dinner in silence. Cade was lost in deep thought while Kate tried to remain quiet but supportive. She knew he was reviewing his options, which were looking grimmer by the moment.

Kate hoped that after they checked into a motel room the silence between them would ease, but Cade remained quiet, brooding. Her worry and anxiety were heightened when Cade lowered himself onto the bed, crossed his arms behind his head and stared up at the ceiling.

Kate stood a few feet inside the door, her hands on her hips. This was taking "I won't be much company" to the limit! He was retreating so far inside himself that it scared her. She thought he had begun to open up to her, but suddenly they were back to square one.

"Cade, talk to me. Please!"

For a moment he continued to stare at the ceiling as if he hadn't heard her. When his eyes did finally rest on her, the icy shards were cutting.

"I thought I didn't have to say a word," he mocked, shifting his attention back to the ceiling.

Kate sank down onto the bed. "Okay, I exaggerated a bit."

"You want me to carry on small talk?" His voice sounded incredulous.

"No. You're not big on small talk. But, Cade, since we left the trailer, I've felt you distancing from me. Don't throw away the communication we've accomplished." She tried to embrace him, but he shrugged away and rose. The action hurt her more than his words, and she bit her lower lip to keep from saying anything else.

Without looking at her, he said in a voice that was as frosty as his eyes, "We begin early tomorrow. You'd better get your sleep." His expression dismissed the idea of a two-way conversation.

Frustrated, Kate got ready for bed, deciding to sleep in her clothes. She didn't think she'd be able to sleep, but soon she dozed fitfully.

The sound of someone moving near the window snapped her eyes open. She propped herself up on her elbows, her eyes quickly adjusting to the darkness in the room. Moonlight streamed through the window. Cade's arm was braced against the frame, his head bowed, resting on his forearm, as he stared out into the night.

She wanted to go to him and wrap her arms around him. She wanted to hold him fiercely and whisper that everything would be all right, his dream would come true—it had to! But Kate did nothing because Cade had stepped effortlessly back into his role of a loner.

When he lifted his free hand and rubbed the back of his neck, Kate could no longer keep quiet. "Cade?"

He said nothing. She wouldn't have known he had even heard her if his hand hadn't stopped for a few seconds. He was choosing to ignore her. The tightness in her throat grew hot and aching.

His head came up. "Kate, I'm sorry. I've hurt you again." His voice faded into the silence and it was several minutes before he continued, "I'm not good at sharing myself, Kate. I didn't even tell Rachel my feelings all those years we were married. Oh, she knew the facts but not the emotions behind them." He turned and sat back on the windowsill. "It wasn't the fact I was a bastard that hurt. It was the rejection. Judd rejected my mother and he rejected me, or so I thought. He made love to Ruth while engaged to Anne. Anne is from a wealthy Texas family. It was her money that gave my father his big start."

"Because of that you're determined to succeed without my help or my family's?"

He nodded once.

"But there's a difference!" Kate sat up in bed and swung her legs to the floor. "Don't you understand I would be investing, not giving you the money?"

"That doesn't matter. You're part of my personal life and I want it to remain that way." He pushed himself upright. "It's almost dawn. Let's get moving."

Kate swallowed the words she was going to say. Cade had a lot on his mind at the moment. But she resolved that she would accept nothing less than being an equal partner in Cade's life. She wasn't the type of woman who could settle for less.

At the well site Kate again watched and waited in the trailer. Nervous, she constantly rubbed her hands together, but they remained clammy.

When the door opened two hours later, she was pouring her fourth cup of coffee. She knew it was Cade. She was afraid to turn around and look at him. Fortifying herself with a deep breath, she pivoted.

His face was absolutely expressionless as he declared, "The hole is dry."

Chapter Twelve

Cade's features tensed into a frown as he pulled his pickup truck onto the dirt road that led to Number Two Weston. He glanced briefly toward Kate and said, "This may take some time."

"Cade Weston, you promised me a picnic lunch and I want a picnic lunch even if it's at seven o'clock tonight."

"Give you an inch, you take a mile and then some," he grumbled good-naturedly, cupping his hand around her neck and pulling her toward him.

After all the trouble over the last few weeks she hoped this problem wasn't too serious. With the first well coming up dry, Cade had had to approach both Howard and Paul for more money to drill the second well. It hadn't been easy but he finally persuaded them to invest in this well, three thousand feet to the west of the first one. Cade felt the first one was on the bottom edge of a pool, whereas he needed his hole at the top of the crest. But which direction from the original well had been a calculated guess.

"Is this serious?" Kate nestled close to him, banishing the past weeks' problems and instead enjoying the sinewy feel of Cade against her.

"Could be. We're losing mud. At the rate Jim quoted it could take another two or three thousand dollars a day to replace the mud. Money I don't have, I might add. My share in this well will be less as it is."

"You won't have to stop drilling, will you?" Concern sounded in her voice.

"I hope not." The frown sliced deeper into his face. "I don't want to have to go back to my investors and ask for more money to drill this well if I can help it."

Cade stopped next to the trailer and climbed down from the cab. Jim spotted him and waved. The tool pusher walked toward Cade, a grave expression on his weathered face.

"How much fluid is the hole taking now?" Cade asked when Jim was within three feet of him.

Jim's sharp gaze flicked to Kate for a brief moment, then back to Cade as he answered gruffly, "Seventy barrels. But we have another problem to complicate matters, I'm afraid. We have gas in the mud."

Cade slammed the palm of his hand against the door of his truck. "Damn!" His frown strengthened into a scowl. "Of all the blasted luck. We're not far from where the pay sand is. You know what to do, Bary. I'll stay until the situation looks better."

Jim made his way back toward the rig floor while Cade said, "Kate, I hate to ask you again, but will you stay in the trailer until this problem is taken care of? This may take all day, but I'd worry about you if you were up on the floor with me. I wish you hadn't talked me into letting you come along. I really thought they'd have the mud problem under control." He attempted a rueful grin but failed. "My only excuse for not thinking rationally is that your presence does things to me that should be outlawed."

"I'm not sorry I'm here even if I have to wait again. I want to be with you, Cade." She brushed her finger down his jawline. "All I'd have done in Denver is clean my house."

He seized her hand and bit lovingly on each fingertip, desire in his eyes. "What I'm thinking right now would shock even those roughnecks."

Kate saw Jim staring at them from the drilling platform. Even from a distance she could feel the man's disapproval. It instantly sobered her. Looking back at Cade, she asked, "What does it mean to have gas in the mud?"

"We already have a bad problem with the loss-circulation, but with the gas, we have to do two entirely opposite procedures to control both problems, which is very difficult. If we can't get rid of the gas I'm afraid we'll take a kick and there will be a blowout." He grasped her arms, his eyes glinting with gravity. "I wish I had a way to get you back to town, Kate. It's going to be a boring day for you."

"Cade, even if you could find a way back for me, I wouldn't leave. We have a date." The resolve in her voice was mirrored in her expression.

Kate waited until Cade was striding toward Jim before making her way inside the trailer. Pouring herself a cup of coffee, she began the long, lonely wait. Cade came into the trailer twice for a cup of coffee, the lines around his mouth and eyes deep with worry and exhaustion. The second time, around five o'clock in the evening, he kissed her briefly and said things were starting to look better. For the first time Kate relaxed, sitting on a cot and leaning back against the wall.

At six-thirty Cade and Jim entered the trailer, some of the strain erased. Jim scowled at her as he went to the coffee urn and grabbed a cup.

Cade smiled his reassurances across the room and said, "I hope you packed some food. I'm starved."

He held his hand out and Kate walked toward him. Cade called over his shoulder as they left the trailer, "I'll be back in a while, Bary."

"I don't think you have to worry, boss. We're only losing twenty barrels of mud now and there's no gas in it."

"Still I'll check once more before I leave for Denver."

Kate shivered at the thought of Jim's open hostility in the trailer. When Cade closed the door, she felt decidedly better.

"I'm sorry about Bary, Kate. He's a damn good foreman, but he believes a lady has no business being at a drilling site."

Kate laughed shakily. "Kinda like a lady has no business being in a position of authority." A tinge of bitterness crept into her voice as she thought of Clayton and Samuel.

Cade had begun to start the truck but stopped and twisted around in the seat to face her. "Is Coleman still giving you a hard time, honey?"

"There are times when he lets his chauvinism show. But actually he's been better. After all, he got what he wanted: power. Cade, let's forget our problems for a few hours and find a spot to eat the food I've prepared.'' Kate realized with the mention of Samuel that she should say something about the phone call from New York.

Grinning, he turned the key in the ignition and pulled away from the well site. "I know just the place and it's not far from here."

"Will it be all right to stop there?"

"I don't think the owner will mind. When this well comes in, he'll be a richer man."

"I like your positive thinking."

"I have to think positive," Cade said seriously. "If it doesn't come in I'll have to work for an oil company and start all over again. It takes a lot of time to get enough collateral for a line of credit. But I won't give up this dream. I've had it for too long. The dream is possible with a little bit of luck."

He parked at the edge of a grove of trees. Cade carried the picnic basket and guided her through the underbrush to the bank of the stream.

"Oh, Cade, this is beautiful."

The stream was small, easily crossed. Holding her hand, he picked his way over some stones to the other side.

After they were settled on the grass and Kate had opened the basket, she asked, "What will the loss-circulation problem mean in terms of your working capital?''

Cade pulled the cork out of the wine bottle and filled two glasses. "If it continues and another problem arises, I'll completely deplete my capital for this well in less than a week."

Her head came up with a start. She wanted to say, "Don't worry. I have the money you'd need." She didn't. Instead she said, "Everything will work out. You'll hit your pay sand within a few days."

Cade's expression was frighteningly solemn. "Today my realism is beginning to win out. A two-hundred-thousand-dollar line of credit is depleted after only two wells. I'm starting to question putting so much into this land lease. But the oil is down there, Kate. I just don't know if I should have gone five hundred feet to the northwest instead of directly west."

Her heart felt heavy with concern. *Either the well will strike oil or it won't,* Kate thought. *No in-betweens for us.*

With her legs drawn up she stared at the water gently rippling over the stones in the streambed. Playing with the cuff of her jeans, she tried to think how to approach the subject of her job offer. The bank in New York wanted her soon. The situation at the Denver Exchange Bank wasn't the best to work under, but for Cade she would.

"Cade, I've been offered a good job at a big bank in New York City."

There was a lengthy silence between them, filled with sounds of nature.

"Do you want me to offer you a guarantee for the future, Kate? I can't. My future is too uncertain to ask anyone to share it with me." His voice was strangely void of emotions, but his feelings were conveyed by the deep slashing lines in his expression.

Maybe that was what she wanted, a guarantee that he would marry her. She realized her patience was wearing out.

Cade took her face within his hands and forced her to look at him. "I love you, Kate. But I can't commit myself until I know where my future lies."

"Cade, all I want is you. I have a good job. I have enough money for us." The second she spoke the words she knew she had said the wrong thing.

Cade yanked his hands away from her face as if he had touched a red-hot stove. His expression contorted with fury. "My God, woman, I don't want your damn money! Don't you understand that?" He strode to the stream, his arms stiff at his sides, his posture rigid. He hung his head and gazed down at the water.

She had pushed him into a corner at a time when he had a lot on his mind. She would lose him completely if she pursued it. "Cade, I didn't mean to say that about the money. It's been a long day and we're both just tired and hungry. Come on and eat. You'll know about your well within the next few days.''

Cade massaged his neck, something he did when he was tense. ''Why did you bring up the job offer, Kate?'' He turned slowly, his eyes blank. His years of experience at hiding beneath a facade were utilized now.

''I have to give them an answer by the end of this month. It's an excellent opportunity, Cade, I won't deny that. But the thing I want the most in this world is you.''

''In order to come up with my share of the money, Paul Carson personally loaned me fifteen thousand dollars. So it's not just my line of credit at stake here.''

''Oh, Cade, why?'' The question barely got past her lips.

''I was short that much for a third interest in the well. I know it's a gamble, but I didn't come all this way for only a fourth interest.''

''I see,'' she murmured. She busied herself with laying out the food. She felt completely shut out of his life and it hurt. It was fine for him to borrow from strangers or acquaintances, but not from someone who loved him?

"Kate, please trust me. I have to do this my way." His voice was a husky whisper. He knelt in front of her and took her hands in his.

"I'm trying, Cade. But we're not Judd and Anne. Your pride could destroy us."

"My self-respect is important to me. It's part of who I am. I can't change overnight, Kate."

"We'd better eat," she said quickly, offering him a travesty of a smile.

In silence they ate their lunch, even though it was seven at night and the sun was down. Kate had roasted a hen the day before, and its flavor was delicious, but she wasn't hungry. Cade, too, ate very little. The tension between them was almost tangible.

Again without a word they quickly packed up the basket and walked back to the truck. Fifteen minutes later they were at the well site, now lit with floodlights. Cade parked next to the trailer.

"Cade, I've never seen a drilling rig. Since all you're going to do is check on the well and then leave, may I come, too?"

"Okay, but if there's any problem, you wait in the trailer again."

From his truck bed Cade grabbed two hard hats, gave one to Kate, and together they walked toward the drilling platform. Kate followed him up the stairs that led to the raised rotary-rig floor. There were several men working at various jobs at the rotary table and drill stem, where the pipe was being run down into the hole. Jim was standing next to the driller at the console when Cade crossed the floor to him.

Kate stopped to accustom herself to all the equipment and noise. Looking up, she noticed a man coming down from the monkey board, a platform near the top of the rig. Seeing the complicated drilling process up close made Kate understand even better the enormous cost it took to explore for oil and natural gas.

"Is everything holding?" Cade asked Jim.

"Yeah." The tool pusher's intense regard strayed to Kate. His hostile eyes questioned her presence on the rig floor. Turning back to Cade, he continued, "We're not losing any more mud, and there isn't any more gas."

The set of Cade's shoulders relaxed. "Good. I'm heading back to Denver. If anything comes up call me immediately. I want to know about even the slightest change in the condition of the well."

"Will do, boss."

Cade was guiding Kate toward the stairs when the night air was pierced with a loud horn sounding above the noise of the drilling. Cade spun around.

Jim was already shouting orders. "Pick up the kelly joint, then shut in the BOPs."

Kate clutched at Cade's arm. "What's happening?"

"The well's flowing," he answered her, then to Jim he asked, "What's the pit-mud-volume indicator say?"

"We took a twenty-barrel kick and we'll have to circulate it out."

"Check the choke manifold and make sure all the valves are set properly."

Jim turned to a roughneck and ordered the man to go below into the cellar and check everything out.

Cade watched the roughneck disappear below the drilling platform. This was it! Everything he'd worked toward was coming true. He smiled down broadly at Kate and laid his hand over hers. But the smile died on his lips as the floor began to vibrate.

"Cade?" Kate's hold on his arm tightened.

"It's okay. The gas is getting closer to the surface. The man below is checking to make sure everything is tight on the blowout preventer."

A high-pitched scream ripped the air; the floor shook. In the next second an explosion thundered beneath Cade's feet, and he was galvanized into motion.

He shoved Kate toward the stairs, shouting above the pandemonium around them, "Get the hell out of here. Now!"

Kate stumbled and grasped the railing. Fear gripped her. The earth trembled and rocked as if an earthquake had hit the well site. "But, Cade..."

"No buts, Kate. Move!" His tone was like a whip prodding her to leave.

Roughnecks scrambled off the rig, one knocking into Kate as he flew down the stairs. Regaining her balance, she covered her mouth and nose with a quaking hand. The odor of raw gas assaulted her, shocking her into action. Halfway to the trailer she looked back, but Cade was nowhere to be seen. In a panic, she started back toward the rig when Jim grabbed her arm, a wall between her and Cade.

"Let me go," she said through gritted teeth, looking up defiantly into his stormy eyes.

"Look, lady, I'm just following orders. Cade told me to make sure everyone was safely away from the rig, especially you."

"Cade may need me. I have to go back." Confusion and fright numbed her.

"Lady, all hell is breaking loose up there. Gas is blowing everywhere. He's going after Lawson. You can't help him."

"No! Not Cade!" The scream was wrenched from the depths of her soul. Not her Cade going down into that hellhole!

Kate had time only to glance quickly at the rig before the tool pusher propelled her forward. She dug her heels into the ground, resisting him.

A rational thread clung to her mind and she said in a relatively calm voice, "I have no intention of being near that thing if it goes. But how can *you* leave him there without any help?" Her voice and eyes accused Jim Bary.

"It was an order, lady, and you don't argue with Cade. He saw no need for more than one person to go below, to..."

The tool pusher's voice faded, but his meaning was clear. *To risk his life for the man trapped below the drilling platform,* she finished silently.

Kate struggled to free herself, but the man who had been openly hostile toward her and who held her so tightly was determined that she would accompany him away from the drilling platform— away from Cade. In the cold, harsh reality of the next few minutes Kate, safe inside the trailer, realized she might never see Cade again.

The memory of Thomas's skiing accident pummeled her, and she couldn't get a decent breath. She couldn't go through that again; she knew the agony of losing the man she loved.

Kate was oblivious to all the commotion, her heart and mind encased in ice. Her eyes were trained on the door as she prayed vehemently that the next time it opened Cade would stride through it. But the door remained closed.

With each passing minute she felt part of her die. The waiting seemed an eternity, a living nightmare. Her mind whirled with the events that had just occurred on the rig floor.

She moved to brush her fingers through her hair and encountered the hard plastic of the hard hat she still wore. Was this hat enough to protect Cade? No, not if some small spark ignited the gas bursting out of the hole. Nothing would protect him.

Kate buried her face in her hands, shudders racking her body. Pain spread up from her burning lungs into her throat. Anxiety twisted her insides.

Kate bolted to her feet. She couldn't stand it any longer. She had taken only three steps toward the door when a hand restrained her. She yanked her arm from the tool pusher's grasp. Nothing would keep her from at least waiting outside, where she would have a clear view of the rig. Her reserve of strength and quiet authority were firmly intact when she rounded Jim Bary, her face feverish with an intent purpose.

"Lady, I just called the police and the well-control specialists. You must stay inside. If the wind shifts, we have to leave here." Strain had taken its toll on him, his weathered features even sharper and lashed with deep grooves.

"What about Cade? I won't budge without him. I don't care what you say."

The tool pusher was about to argue with her when the door slammed open. Relief swept through her. Cade stood in the doorway, covered with mud and carrying the injured roughneck in his arms.

The impact of Cade's near death caused her knees to buckle, and she collapsed against the table, clutching it for support. Her torment was betrayed by her ashen face. Her wide blue eyes fixed on Cade, who was barking out a series of orders, the first being to call an ambulance for the roughneck.

Cade carefully laid the unconscious man on a cot, then spoke to Jim. "Lawson was knocked up against the substructure, but he's alive. Thank God for that."

"The fire fighters and police are on their way. They'll want to see you."

Cade nodded, then turned toward Kate. His eyes softened when they rested upon her pale face and saw her frightened look. "I'm okay. I want you to call your brother and have him come for you. I want you out of here, especially if that well catches fire. No arguments, Kate. I can't handle it right now." Defeat blended with his strong voice, causing it to shake slightly on the last sentence.

His desperation singed her very core, and Kate knew she would do as he said. She had no other choice. "I'll go, Cade." He moved to go outside when she suddenly added in a frantic voice, "I love you. Please be careful."

Cade glanced back over his shoulder at her, his eyes shadowed with grief as though he were in mourning. "I'll be as careful as possible. But I won't kid you, Kate. That rig could go up in a raging inferno. That was all I thought about when I went down after Lawson. It's very sobering to see your life flash before your eyes. Call your brother now."

Then he was gone, the door closing behind him. Seeing the defeat in Cade splintered her tattered emotions and laid them about her in hundreds of slivers.

"Greg, you don't have to stay any longer. I'm fine," Kate said in a voice that transmitted her deep worry for Cade. She turned from the window, letting the drape fall back into place.

"I'm not leaving until you hear from Cade. I remember us staying up all night as kids. Do you remember that one Christmas when we woke Mom and Dad four times before they finally went downstairs?"

Preoccupied, Kate nodded as she walked to the couch, ran her finger along a cushion, then restlessly turned and strode back to the window that overlooked the street. No red pickup truck. *No Cade.*

"Do you remember when we went water-skiing and you saw that snake? You didn't ski for weeks after that."

She pressed her forehead against the cool glass and said absently, "Yes."

Greg's hand lay heavily upon her shoulder. "Sit down, and I'll get you a cup of coffee."

"I can't drink another cup, Greg. What's happening out there? What if the well caught on fire and he was in the middle of it all?"

Greg kneaded the taut cords of her shoulders and neck. "He'll be all right, Kate. He has to stay until everything is under control. That will take time. You should try to get some rest."

Kate spun around. "Rest! How can you say that? I'm so tied up in knots it hurts. I keep remembering when the doctor told me Thomas was dead. Cade risked his life last night and I could have lost him just like that." She snapped her fingers, all her anxiety and concern in her expression. "I still might." Her voice cracked.

"He did what he had to do. Cade isn't a man who could have walked away from someone trapped like that."

Her eyes burned; her body was so physically exhausted that she wasn't sure what was holding her up. "That's what I love about him and I wouldn't expect anything less from him. But . . ."

"Sit down, Kate, before you fall down." Greg's voice was stern. "Standing guard at the window isn't doing any good. It won't make Cade arrive any sooner."

Kate sat on the couch, where she and Cade had sat many times. Staring down at the empty place next to her, she imagined Cade taking her into his arms. At that moment she came to a decision. His near death made her realize she couldn't live like this any longer. If he loved her, nothing should stand in the way of their getting married. She couldn't stand to be apart from him for another second.

The next few hours passed one slow second at a time. Kate heard Greg talk, his words not registering. It was just noise that filled the void and he knew that, so he didn't demand any response from her.

When someone finally rang the doorbell, Kate flew off the couch and threw open the door. When she saw Greg's campaign manager, Kate almost screamed with frustration.

"You have to be at an important meeting in half an hour, Greg."

When Greg started to tell his campaign manager to go on without him, Kate said, "I don't need a baby-sitter. This is important to your career. I'll go into the office, so you can go on to the meeting."

"Call in sick, Kate. You're in no condition to work today and you know it." Greg walked to the phone and picked up the receiver for her.

"Older brothers always think they can tell you what to do," Kate grumbled, knowing Greg was right. Dialing the bank, she told her secretary she wouldn't be in that day.

After the call Greg headed for the front door, saying, "I have to protect my life savings in that bank. I don't want you to do something crazy and loan it all out."

"Not with Samuel breathing down my neck."

Greg opened the door. There, standing in the doorway, was Cade, poised and ready to knock. Kate stood transfixed as Greg spoke a few words to Cade, then left and Cade entered her house. Her legs wouldn't function. She collapsed against the back of the couch, her eyes on Cade as he wearily walked toward her. Exhaustion was stamped on his face. Mud was still caked on his clothes.

His arms went around her and he held her, his heart hammering. Kate ran her hands over him to make sure he was real, not a figment of her imagination.

"Oh, you feel so good." He buried his face in her hair.

The night before, he hadn't known if he would ever hold her again, and now she was in his arms. It was almost too much. He hoped to God he never had to live through another night like that one. His thoughts were swirling at such a high speed that he couldn't grasp any one single thought. He was utterly drained emotionally and physically.

"Cade, come and sit down." Kate helped him to the couch.

"But look at me, Kate." He waved his hand down the length of his dirty clothes.

"My couch can be cleaned. You need to get off your feet. I'll get you a cup of coffee, then you can tell me what happened."

Kate hurried into the kitchen and prepared a new pot of coffee. When she reentered the living room, though, Cade was asleep on her couch. She knelt down by him, her hand lightly touching the tawny hair near his ear. She brushed her lips across his mouth, wishing she could lie next to him. She covered him with a blanket and sat in the chair to watch him sleep. It was a comforting sight to see him in her living room, safe.

* * *

Hours later, as Kate was clearing away the supper dishes, Cade came from her bathroom, shaved and cleaned. They had talked little of the future or the well. She wasn't sure how to bring the subject up, but she didn't want Cade to worry about the financing of the well. Lending him the money was the one thing she could do to ease his problems; she just had to convince him and pray his pride wouldn't stand in the way of his accepting her help.

Exhaustion lingered in the grim lines of his expression as he faced her in the living room. "I have to get back to the well. I just talked to Jim, and the well-control specialists need to see me."

"May I come?"

"Stay here and rest. I don't know how long I'll be. It's safe now, but I'd feel better if you stayed here."

"What happened last night?" she asked finally.

"A valve failed on the casing head below the blowout preventer. After a few hours the pipe in the hole bridged off and it was safe to move in. It never caught fire, thank God. There was little structural damage, but it will be weeks fishing out the stuck pipe and getting the well back in operation, if we can even do that."

Kate knew by the bleak look in his eyes that he was thinking of the cost. She stepped closer until they were inches away from each other. "Cade, I want to lend you the money."

"Kate, please, not now." His fingers tangled themselves in his hair as he rubbed the back of his neck.

"Cade, there will never be a good time. What's mine is yours. That's the only way I'll have it. You don't need to go back to Paul and Howard." She reached out to touch him, but he moved away.

Anger glittered in his brown eyes. "Don't back me up against a wall. We've been through this before. I won't take a dime of your money."

Her heart stopped beating for a few seconds. She couldn't get enough air. "I have to have more than just part of you. Until you let go of your past, you aren't ready for a future with me."

For a moment he stared at her, his eyes narrow. "This is emotional blackmail, Kate."

"Call it what you want. You don't have to go to outsiders for something I can give you. You won't have to worry about the money, Cade. Please accept my help."

His shoulders sagged. "I can't, Kate," he answered in a throaty whisper, then pivoted and strode toward the door.

In shock, Kate watched him leave, not knowing if he would ever come back. Her eyes were wide and dry. There was no emotion left inside her even to cry.

Chapter Thirteen

The ringing sound reached into his sleep-deprived mind and aroused Cade from his semiconscious state. He rubbed his face, feeling the roughness of two days' growth of beard. Stumbling out of bed, he glanced down to make sure he was decent before heading for his front door. *I must look like death warmed over,* he thought as he swung the door open.

He had seen Anne Masters only a few times, but he would never forget what she looked like, especially at this moment. She was a vision of softness in a pale-rose angora sweater dress with a gently draping neckline and long sleeves.

As he stared at her, trying to cover his shock at seeing her, he realized he held no ill feelings toward his father's wife. She had a quiet, sophisticated beauty. Lisa will look like this when she's older, he thought.

Anne smiled, easing some of the strain. "May I come in, Cade?"

He blinked, his mind working more slowly than usual. Stepping aside, he mumbled, "I'm sorry. Yes." He glanced down at his faded clothes and wished he'd changed as well as shaved.

In the middle of his living room Anne turned, her movements graceful and poised. Her honey-blond hair, streaked with gold and white, fell in soft waves, barely brushing her shoulders. It added to the illusion of femininity and vulnerability, but like Lisa, Anne had an inner strength that had supported her through some hard years.

"I called several times and came by yesterday, but you weren't here. I hope I haven't picked a bad time." Her voice was cool and soft.

Cade tried to bring order to his tousled hair. "I've been in the field for the past few days. I just got back an hour ago. Please have a seat." He waved his arm toward the couch. "Is something wrong with Lisa . . . or Judd?" He'd stopped pretending that Judd Masters didn't interest him.

Anne stood for a moment, trying to decide whether to sit or remain on her feet. Cade knew the second she made up her mind. Her tiny frown disappeared, and the satinlike skin on her face smoothed. She sank onto the couch in one elegant movement, placing her clutch purse in her lap. When she raised her jade-green eyes, Cade folded his long length into a chair across from her. Their eyes met, silently agreeing this meeting would be on totally equal terms.

Anne's emotions were carefully concealed behind a polite mask. Cade had seen that same expression on Lisa's face; often it hid a troubled countenance he was learning to recognize.

"Everything is fine with Lisa and Judd." Her pause was slight, but the quick rise of her chest indicated her nervousness. "Lisa and I had a talk a few days ago and we decided I should approach you. Judd and I are renewing our marriage vows at four this afternoon. It will be a small ceremony held at the ranch. I want you to attend."

Surprise widened Cade's dark eyes. "Did Judd ask you to come?"

"Please hear me out." A faint smile edged Anne's mouth before she continued, "He doesn't know anything about it. You know your father well enough to realize he wouldn't send someone else to do his job."

Her casual reference to Judd as his father jolted Cade. "Why are you here?"

"Because Judd is too proud to ask you himself. Our marriage wasn't made in heaven, but now after thirty-five years we are finally happy. Judd doesn't give easily and he won't change completely, but he's a different man now. Facing death makes a person look at things differently."

Cade studied the coffee table between them. Anne was right, but sometimes even looking at things differently took time. He'd been thinking a lot about Kate and what she had said to him. He even wanted to call her, but he wasn't ready to see her. He still had some things to work out in his mind.

"You knew about me from the beginning." Cade lifted his eyes to Anne's face.

"Yes, but Judd didn't know I did. There were times after Lisa was born when I would catch him looking at her. I would see such longing in his eyes. I knew he was thinking of his son and the fact that I couldn't have any more children. He wanted you, Cade, but circumstances kept you two apart. I know Judd has faults, but there's goodness in him. We want you to be there this afternoon as part of the family."

"I don't know." Cade rolled his shoulders to relieve some of the stiffness of days spent mostly on his feet. "I haven't slept in over forty-eight hours. I . . ."

"It's only nine. I'll leave and let you get your sleep, and you can think about what I said when you wake up. In your mind Judd may not deserve a second chance, and you may be right. But I do know Judd loves his children. He's just not very good at showing it."

Stunned, Cade remained sitting as Anne rose and walked toward the front door. He had never thought of Judd's demanding attention as being love. He had never thought of himself as Judd's son but as a possession to be ruled.

"Cade, everyone makes mistakes," Anne said before closing the door after her.

His throat closed. *Mistakes. Oh, God, I've made my share of those lately. Is Judd another one of my mistakes?*

His dark eyes shone with unshed tears as he stared at the place Anne had sat. Nothing. That was what his life was, lonely as hell. For a while it hadn't been, with Kate.

In a week they would resume drilling, but there was no guarantee they would strike oil. And if they did, he would be richer, but he would have nothing. His life would still be empty. Kate had shown him what a life full of love was like, and he had walked out on her. He must be mad!

His throat tightened more and a tear slid down his cheek. He was so damn tired. He was weary of fighting nature, his past, his father, his feelings.

Collapsing back in the chair, he gazed up at the ceiling.

Long moments slipped by; Cade's mind was blank with fatigue. Finally he shoved himself to his feet and trudged toward his bedroom. He couldn't make any decisions until he had had some rest. Falling into bed, he was instantly asleep.

"It's your pride. It will destroy us." Kate's words bombarded him. Her eyes stabbed him with silent recriminations. "We love each other, but you can't let go of the past. You don't want your father to dominate you, yet he rules your every move."

"No!" Cade shot upright in bed, sweat covering his body. Sucking in deep breaths, he tried to steady the beat of his heart, but like the unvarying pitch of an emergency frequency it drummed its message into his brain. *Your damn pride will destroy you.*

His gaze flew to the bedside clock. It was three. He didn't have much time if he was to make the ceremony. He walked into the bathroom, where he shaved and showered. He owed it to himself to see Judd. Then maybe he would be free to go to Kate.

Dressed in a navy-blue suit, Cade left his house with barely enough time to get to the ranch. His hands were cold as he held the steering wheel in an unrelenting grip. He had never been to the ranch, but he knew exactly where it was. He had often been by the turnoff and several times almost directed his truck up the dirt road.

But something had always held him back. Now, as he paused at the entrance, he realized that he had never felt as if he had the right. This ranch had belonged to Judd's other life—a life forbidden to Cade.

Seconds slid into minutes, and yet Cade couldn't bring himself to put his truck into drive. He knew if he didn't see Judd he had no right to go to Kate. His hand wavered above the shift, trembling, the old familiar emotions warring with new tentative ones that Cade hadn't become accustomed to yet.

He rested his forehead on the steering wheel, his fingers biting into his palms. How could he even think he and his father could settle anything? So much had happened over the years that couldn't be changed in one afternoon. He was reaching out for something he couldn't have. He was asking to be rejected. Would he ever learn?

Years ago he had dreamed of having a father who would do things with him, love him. Then came the dream about his own oil company—and the most important dream of all, Kate.

He brought his head up with a jerk and slapped his palm against the steering wheel. He had to start somewhere. He had to come to terms with his father in order to get on with his life.

With an unwavering purpose Cade put the truck into drive. His mind barely acknowledged the fenced-in stretches of field. His thoughts centered on what he would do when he arrived at the house. He was as nervous as a boy on his first date.

He was raising his hand to knock on the door when Lisa swung it open, a bright smile on her face. He returned her smile and stepped through into his father's house for the first time.

Lisa placed her hand on his arm in gentle support. "I'm glad you could come, Cade. It means a lot to me to have you here."

Words eluded him; feelings long denied were emerging. He silently imparted his confusion as he covered her hand with his, and Lisa led him into the living room, where a small gathering was already seated.

"We were waiting for you." Lisa sat down next to Cade and lifted her hand to signal for the organist to begin.

"You're very sure of yourself."

Silent laughter filled Lisa's gray eyes, making them seem almost silver. "I think I'm beginning to know my brother quite well. You could have said no to me but not to my mother. She has her ways."

"I didn't realize my sister was so devious."

Organ music permeated the air and Cade automatically tensed. Soon his father would appear, and Cade's doubts assailed him. Part of him demanded he leave immediately; another part commanded he stay. Lisa, taking his hand within hers, settled the matter. There was nothing but loneliness in his old life. He wanted more and this was the path he must take.

Judd and Anne entered the living room and walked arm in arm toward the minister. Anne's earlier vision of softness was accentuated by the flowing silk dress of ivory that emphasized her petite frame. Judd towered over her by a good foot, the complete contrast to Anne with his dark features and muscular build.

There was a moment during the ceremony when Cade wished that his mother was standing next to Judd. But reality didn't allow that wish to stay long in his mind. That dream had died long ago, the day he had discovered who his father was. His mother hadn't wanted to tell him, but when he was eleven, she could no longer evade his questions. His life had changed that day, because with the knowledge of who his father was came the realization that they would never be a family. That night he had cried; then his emotions had shattered, the remains buried deep inside.

With a detached coolness he watched Judd and Anne kiss at the end of the ceremony. His withdrawal was a protective gesture, but strangely none of the expected pain touched him. It didn't bother him to see his father with Anne, and he marveled at that insight. He felt some of the chains of the past slip away.

When Judd began to greet his guests, his dark gaze immediately found Cade's. Judd's eyes brightened, and for that instant, Cade felt as though he shared something special with his father. Someone spoke to Judd and his attention was reluctantly pulled away.

Lisa squeezed Cade's hand. "Are you all right?"

For a few seconds Cade continued to stare at his father. Then, mentally shaking himself, he looked at his sister. "I'm fine, Lisa."

"I had lunch with Kate yesterday."

Every sense vibrated with the mention of Kate's name. "How is she?"

"She seemed preoccupied. She wouldn't talk about you at all. What happened?"

Two months ago Lisa would never have asked that question, and he wouldn't have answered her. "I walked away from her because I wouldn't accept her money for the well. I was determined to do this totally on my own. You know, the island among men."

"Do you love her?"

"Oh, God, yes. But, Lisa, you sometimes never realize how much until you've lost it."

Lisa smiled. "You haven't lost. Remember, half of your genes are Judd's and he never admits defeat."

Cade laughed. "I'd forgotten. Then you recommend relentless pursuit?"

"By all means."

Cade glanced toward his father. "Well, it's time for me to congratulate the happy couple."

"Will you mean it?"

"Half of my genes are Judd's. Do you think I would say something I didn't mean?"

"No."

But as Cade approached Judd and Anne, he was anxious. This wouldn't be easy.

Anne smiled at him and said, "I'm glad you came, Cade."

The warmth in her regard alleviated some of the awkwardness of the situation. "I wanted to congratulate you. I couldn't the first time around." Another link in the chain fell away.

Judd was silent, his expression unreadable, while Anne said, "Thank you. That means a lot to the both of us. Now, if you'll excuse me, I have some guests to see to."

"Did you mean it, Cade?" Judd asked when Anne had left them alone.

Cade looked his father directly in the eyes. "Yes."

The wariness in Judd's gaze vanished; the tenseness in his shoulders disappeared. "Do you have time to talk alone in my study?"

"Yes."

Judd was stopped once on his way to the study by a guest, but he quickly extracted himself from the conversation. Cade watched his father and acknowledged the resemblance between them. They had the same tall, muscular build, dark brown eyes, strong, aggressive features.

When they were finally in the study, Cade surveyed the room that was Judd's favorite place in the house. Done in warm tones, the room looked comfortable and inviting with burl-walnut paneling and buff leather chairs and couch. A plush champagne-colored carpet lent a lightness to the room that contrasted with the darkness of the paneling. Bookshelves, filled with well-read books, lined one wall.

What drew Cade's attention was a tarnished brass sculpture on a three-foot pedestal near the stone fireplace. A horse stood with its front legs locked while his rider had flipped a cow over on its back and was tying the animal's legs. It was an unusual western sculpture, symbolizing work and action, two things that Judd was known for.

"Why did you come today?" Judd walked to the bar in the corner and fixed himself a drink, lifting the bottle in offer to Cade.

Cade shook his head. He heard the cautious tone in Judd's voice and knew his father was as uneasy as he was. "I'm not sure. I've never heard your side of the story and I suddenly realized it was important to me to hear it."

"My side?" Judd laughed, no amusement in the sound. "I'm certainly not blameless in this situation. I've made some mistakes I've paid dearly for. I loved your mother in my own way. We were friends. But when I went away to college and met Anne I knew she was the one I wanted to marry, all the while knowing that Ruth was waiting for me back in Denver. I didn't marry Anne for her money. It helped us, but I worked damned hard to get where I am today." Judd stared at the amber contents of his glass, then tilted it to his lips and drank.

The pain touched Cade as he listened to his father's explanation. Cade strode to the bar and filled a glass with whiskey, downing half in one gulp. It burned a path down his throat and relieved some of the anguish.

"When I came home from college on vacation, I couldn't completely let go of Ruth. I tried but the words always lodged in my throat. I've paid many times over for that mistake. I've never forgiven myself, even though Ruth has. She never asked anything of me—not even money to help with you—except one thing. She wanted me to leave you and her alone. I realize now my visits that first year were destroying her. I had to respect her plea.''

Judd's voice faltered and he swallowed convulsively. ''Giving you up was the first unselfish thing I ever did. And it was the one time I shouldn't have. But it was what Ruth wanted, and I felt she deserved at least that much from me.''

The last hurt was washed away, and Cade was free of the past. He was his own man now, no longer a prisoner of circumstances beyond his control.

Judd finished his drink and set the glass on the bar, his gaze seeking Cade's. ''I wanted you as my son so badly that when I began reading about you when you were playing football, I couldn't stay away any longer. I tried to avoid Ruth, but I wanted to know my son, to share in his life.'' His mouth turned upward in a self-mocking grin. ''When you wouldn't have anything to do with me, I thought I could convince you. I did all the wrong things. So I followed your life from afar, hoping one day that the truth would be known but realizing I wouldn't say anything because of Anne and Lisa. I had already hurt enough people.''

Judd paused, clearing his throat. ''I love you, son, and I want to acknowledge you to the world, if you'll let me.''

Cade stared at the empty bottom of his glass; his heart ached with a remembered hurt. "I remember fighting with a kid at school because he called me a bastard. That night I lay in bed, unable to sleep, and dreamed about you saying those very words to me. I prayed so hard for you to walk through my door to declare your love that I didn't sleep the whole night." He lifted his gaze to Judd's, Cade's eyes burning intently. "Being illegitimate wasn't the worst thing in the world, but I allowed it to color everything. I'm tired of all the half truths and want the slate wiped clean. I've always wanted a father and that has never changed."

Following Cade's admission there was a silence, a soothing, healing silence as each assessed the other. Cade took a step toward his father, holding his hand out.

Judd looked at the offered hand and started to shake it, then hugged his son. "I'm glad you came. I married a wise woman." His voice was rough, barely audible as he pulled back. "Did you win the fight?"

Cade threw back his head and laughed, cherishing the moment. "Yes, I did. The kid never called me a bastard again."

"Good. Will you stay for dinner?"

"No. I have to see Kate."

"Lisa told me you two weren't seeing each other."

"That will change if I can convince her to have me."

"I hope you do a better job with her than I did with you," Judd said with a laugh. "If things work out, bring Kate back with you. We'll eat at eight. There's always a place at my table for you."

Cade strode toward the door, saying, "I'd like that."

When Cade's hand was on the knob of the door, Judd called out, "Will you develop those oil leases for me now?"

Cade glanced back, amusement in his eyes. "I will if my well comes in. Then we can be equal partners. That's the only way I'll do it."

"Where in the hell did you get your stubbornness?"

"From you, of course."

Kate tried to keep herself occupied in order not to think of Cade, but the harder she tried, the less she succeeded. Everywhere she turned there was a reminder of him. She finally had to acknowledge that she was a one-man woman and that would never change.

Over the past three days she had almost called Cade four times, once having allowed the phone to ring. Thank goodness he hadn't been home, she thought as she walked into the kitchen and opened her refrigerator, trying to decide what to eat for dinner. Finally she decided to go on a diet.

There were times she was disgusted with herself. She had no pride when it came to Cade. But then, he had enough for the both of them.

The loud pounding at her front door halted her halfway across her living room. Somehow she knew it was Cade.

"May I come in, Kate?"

"What if I said no?"

"I'd come in anyway. I have to talk to you."

"Then why bother to ask?" She moved out of his way, feigning boredom.

When he slammed the door shut, she faced him, her anger building. She was trying to piece her life back together. How dare he come back and disrupt it all over again! *Who in the world are you trying to fool, Kathleen Dole? Without Cade you're only half a person.*

"Okay. You have one minute to say what's on your mind." Her stance was defiant, her eyes blazing. This time things had to be settled between them because she couldn't continue living in an upside-down world. She had to have all of Cade.

"I need twenty thousand dollars for the well. When can you have the money ready for me?"

"Banking hours are from nine to five, Mr. Weston," she replied crisply, but her mounting anger was crumbling. She resisted the urge to walk into his embrace. Too much was at stake to give in too quickly.

"I'm asking for a *personal* loan between you and me, with a stipulation attached."

"What?" The tenseness eased from her body, and she leaned back against the door.

"I want you to marry me as soon as possible."

"Are you the collateral?"

"This will be a partnership right down the middle."

"What if your well doesn't come in, Cade?"

"Then I'll start over with you at my side. I love you, Kate. It's that simple." He opened his arms wide, but his expression was full of uncertainty.

Her features relaxed into a half smile. "I can have the money for you tomorrow." She moved into the circle of his arms.

"I take it that's a yes." Cade returned the smile, his eyes alight with happiness.

Kate nodded as his mouth came down upon hers. His kiss renewed the deep bond between them. His tongue pushed between her slightly parted lips and touched hers, hot and moist.

His breath warmed her neck; his tongue flicked over the sensitive skin. "I've missed you so much, Kate. Can you take an absolute fool? Sometimes I amaze myself at what a slow learner I am."

"Next time you stray I'll be there to set you straight." Kate toyed with the top button of his blue shirt, finally slipping it out of its hole.

Cade nestled Kate to him as they walked into the living room. "I saw my father today. Judd and Anne renewed their marriage vows."

"And you went?"

"Yes."

"Oh, Cade, I'm glad—I think. How did it go?" She tipped her head back to look up into his eyes. There was no aloof barrier in them now, only happiness, love, desire.

"It was a beginning. I guess you could say that after thirty-five years I finally have a father."

On the couch Cade drew her to him and told her about the ceremony and his meeting with Judd. "He asked me to bring you for dinner."

"What time?" Her fingers played with the second button on his shirt.

"Eight."

"That gives us an hour. Can you think of anything to pass the time?" The second button was freed and Kate went to work on the third one.

"Don't you want to hear about Number Two Weston? After all, you're an investor now." Humor spiced his voice as he watched her slowly undress him.

"Oh, sure," she murmured absently.

"The well can be salvaged, and we're fishing out the bridged pipe right now. When that's through, we'll start drilling—*Kate!*"

Her tongue was leaving a wet trail over his chest, circling one of his male nipples, then the other. His raggedly inhaled breath brought her head up. "Go on, I'm listening."

"But I'm not talking. You say we have an hour? Judd will understand if we're a little late."

She smiled mischievously. "Why would we be late?"

"To seal our loan—" Cade pushed her back on the couch, imprisoning her with his body and the dark passion in his gleaming eyes "—with this." And he proceeded to seal not only their loan, but their future, and their dreams of tomorrow.

COMING NEXT MONTH

FORGIVE AND FORGET—Tracy Sinclair
Rand worked for the one man Dani hated—her grandfather. And though
Dani knew it was just Rand's job to entertain her, she found herself falling
in love with him.

HONEYMOON FOR ONE—Carole Halston
Jack Adams was more than willing to do the imitation bridegroom act, but
he didn't want to stop with an imitation, and Rita wasn't willing
to comply. She wanted someone serious and stable, and Jack was
anything but.

A MATCH FOR ALWAYS—Maralys Wills
Jon was a player without a coach; Lindy was a coach without a player.
They made an unbeatable team so it was only natural they would find each
other. Suddenly tennis wasn't the only game they were playing.

ONE MAN'S LOVE—Lisa Jackson
When Stacey agreed to help Nathan Sloan with his daughter, she didn't
realize that the father would be the biggest puzzle—and cause the
most problems.

SOMETHING WORTH KEEPING—Kathleen Eagle
Brenna was unsure about returning to the Black Hills, but nonetheless she
was excited to compete against Cord O'Brien. She was confident she could
win the horse race, but she might lose her heart in the process.

BETWEEN THE RAINDROPS—Mary Lynn Baxter
Cole Weston was hired to prove that Beth Loring was an unfit mother. But
how could he build a case against this woman when he found himself
falling head over heels in love with her?

Silhouette Desire

**Available
January 1987**

NEVADA
SILVER

The third book in the exciting
Desire Trilogy by Joan Hohl.

The Sharp brothers are back, along with
sister Kit...and Logan McKittrick.

Kit's loved Logan all her life and, with a little
help from the silver glow of a Nevada night,
she must convince the stubborn rancher that
she's a woman who needs a man's love—not
the protection of another brother.

Don't miss *Nevada Silver*—Kit and
Logan's story and the conclusion
of Joan Hohl's acclaimed
Desire Trilogy.

Take 4 Silhouette
Special Edition novels
FREE

and preview future books in your home for 15 days!

When you take advantage of this offer, you get 4 Silhouette Special Edition® novels FREE and without obligation. Then you'll also have the opportunity to preview 6 brand-new books —delivered right to your door for a FREE 15-day examination period—as soon as they are published.

When you decide to keep them, you pay just $1.95 each ($2.50 each in Canada) *with no shipping, handling, or other charges of any kind!*

Romance *is* alive, well and flourishing in the moving love stories of Silhouette Special Edition novels. They'll awaken your desires, enliven your senses, and leave you tingling all over with excitement...and the first 4 novels are yours to keep. You can cancel at any time.

As an added bonus, you'll also receive a FREE subscription to the Silhouette Books Newsletter as long as you remain a member. Each issue is filled with news on upcoming books, interviews with your favorite authors, even their favorite recipes.

To get your 4 FREE books, fill out and mail the coupon today!

Silhouette Special Edition®

Silhouette Books, 120 Brighton Rd., P.O. Box 5084, Clifton, NJ 07015-5084